John D. Nesbitt

LEISURE BOOKS NEW YORK CITY

For Rocío

A LEISURE BOOK®

January 2000

Published by

Dorchester Publishing Co., Inc.
276 Fifth Avenue
New York, NY 10001

ISBN 0-8439-4671-7

Printed in the United States of America.

Chapter One

Quinn shifted in the saddle and looked over his shoulder to see if the packhorse was trailing along smoothly. The canvas pack was still riding straight up and balanced, and the dark brown horse moved forward with its smooth, steady walk. Quinn turned back around, adjusted his reins, and settled back into the motion of the saddle horse's walk. As he did so, his gaze moved back ahead of him, scanning the ground and then the trail ahead.

The Wyoming cattle range was not dangerous country, and as far as Quinn knew, he had no one on his backtrail. Nevertheless, he made it a habit to keep his eyes open and moving. Alternately he watched the ground below him and then, with broad sweeps and figure eights, he kept track of the rolling plains country around him. Once in a while he looked back at the packhorse, and on some of those occasions he took a broader look backward at the country he had just passed through.

It was big country, most of it still open range. Earlier in the day he had crossed a railroad that ran east from Orin and Lost Spring to Lusk and beyond, and in the past few days he had seen fences and windmills that also broke up the range. The railroad now lay several miles behind him to the north, and as Quinn looked around him he saw only the dips and rises of grassland with buttes in the distance, to the south and east. Off to his right, beyond where he pictured the North Platte River to be, he saw darker mountains rising above the plains in a blue haze, a full day's ride to the west. They would be the Laramie Mountains.

Bringing his gaze back in to the land ahead of him, Quinn decided to take a few minutes' rest. Now at midday he would find little shade, but a cutbank he saw on the right side of the trail would give a backdrop. Even when he had no sense of danger, Quinn liked to blend into the landscape if he had a choice.

Ordinarily he might have dismounted, but he chose to stay in the saddle. It was a feeling he had, the sense that he might be about to see something. He had had the feeling before, and he had heard other riders talk of seeing an object after having expected it. Some said it was a reflection in the air—a horse and rider, for example, on the other side of a hill. Others said it was a form that a man actually saw but did not register consciously—like a snake moving through a screen of prairie grass. One man Quinn had met, a hunter who spent most of his time in the Bighorn Mountains, said he often saw deer or elk or bear that way because something in the back of his mind told him when he was in the right place and time to see a critter. He said that other talk was just moonglow.

Open country was different from the mountains. Maybe there were such things as reflections, or mirages as they were called. But whatever it was that made Quinn want to stop, it seemed credible, for within a couple of minutes a lone coyote came trotting up over the brow of a low hill. It paused at the crest, looked back over its shoulder, and then moved ahead at a fast walk. It was less than a quarter of a mile away, angling across a broad swale.

Quinn felt the horse shift its weight beneath him, and the coyote must have caught the movement. It jerked into a straight, dead run with its tail streaming out behind. The fleet animal zigged to the left and then back to the right before it disappeared behind a rise of grassland.

Quinn moved the horses forward. Whatever the coyote had seen might be worth taking a look at.

He headed for the little swell where the coyote had come across. Before his line of vision cleared the crest, he stopped the horses again. This time he dismounted, and holding the reins and lead rope with his right hand, he walked slowly up the hill until the country beyond came into view. He saw nothing in the near distance, so he led the horses to the top of the rise and paused there. Standing with his back close to the horses, he laid his left hand flat on the front of his hat brim and scanned the country.

Off to the southeast, less than a mile away, he saw a dark object against the silver green of the midsummer plains. It was moving in Quinn's direction at a three-quarter angle, so he did not get a good view of it either straight-on or in profile. At first it looked like two horsemen, or at least two horses. The shape was too thick to be just one horse. As the party came closer, Quinn distinguished one horse head and neck from another. Then the horses turned and separated into two, and he could see that only the horse on his right carried a rider. Coming closer, the horses turned again. This time Quinn saw the shine of sunlight on saddle leather. The rider was leading a horse with an empty saddle, and he was keeping the animal snubbed close.

Quinn relaxed his gaze. The approaching rider had not changed his course, and he and Quinn had obviously seen each other. Across the quiet prairie, Quinn sensed a hovered understanding that the two riders would meet in a few minutes. Quinn took the occasion to check the cinch on his saddle horse and the lashes on the packhorse. Then he stood as before, facing the oncoming party.

As the horses came within a hundred yards, Quinn saw that the rider was leading the second horse by the reins, which would account for the closeness of the two horses. Fifty yards closer, and Quinn saw the knotted end of reins sticking out from the circled thumb and forefinger of the rider's gloved right hand, like a small bunch of flowers. A rider would hold the reins that way so that a slight pressure from the heel of the hand would control the animal being led.

Both horses were sorrels, common-looking ranch stock. The empty horse had no markings, while the rider's horse had a narrow white blaze to the nose and two white socks in back. Each saddle carried a rope, and the story almost told itself.

"Afternoon," said the rider, raising his gloved left hand to touch his hat brim. His own reins were also tied together, no doubt as a good measure when his right hand was occupied. For the moment of greeting he laid the knotted reins slack against the saddle horn.

"How do you do," Quinn answered. He noticed the man's bright blue eyes and light brown hair.

"Fair enough," said the other man, smiling as he held up both sets of reins. "Took me half the mornin' to catch this horse, but I got 'im, and now I'm headed back."

"Uh-huh." Quinn looked at the horse and back at the stranger. "Bad horse?" As he asked the question, he realized that if the horse were troublesome, the man would probably have it on a rope instead of by the reins.

The other man smiled and shook his head. "Not so bad, really. Just not a very good rider."

"Oh."

"Kid from back east. I wouldn't be surprised if he got his leg broke on this one. He couldn't stand up."

Quinn thought he heard a southern accent in the man's voice, and he sensed the smooth, easy manner he had noticed in so many of the hands who had come up the trail. He squinted and asked, "Did you leave him someplace?"

"Nah. I sent for a wagon first. Then I took out after the horse. He was on a pretty good lope. I figger they must've fed him some good oats one time in Cheyenne, and he wanted to go back."

Quinn gave a short laugh, as he imagined he should. "What outfit do you ride for?"

The man moved his head, motioning westward with his hat. "Lockhart Ranch." Then he nodded at Quinn's outfit. "Passin' through?"

"Lookin' for work."

"Just as good."

Silence hung in the air for a second until Quinn spoke. "Name's Quinn. Travis Quinn. Been up in the Powder River country, and eventually I'd like to drop in on Cheyenne, but I'm in no hurry." Then after a thought he said, "I don't remember any good oats there."

The other man laughed. "I'm Miles Newman," he said. "Most of the time I just go by Newman." He gave a wry smile. "I come up through Cheyenne myself, a while back. Oats were middlin', I'd say."

Quinn nodded.

"You might just as well ride back with me," Newman said. "I don't think that kid's gonna be back on top of a horse for a while, and Sully might could use another hand. At the very least, you could try the grub."

"Sully?"

"Lockhart. Sully Lockhart."

"Uh-huh." Quinn thought for a second. "Worth a try, I guess."

"I'd say." Newman paused and then said, in his easy, smiling manner, "Pleased to meet you, Quinn." He laid his reins against the saddle horn again, shifted the other reins from his right hand to his left, and crossed his right arm down in front of him to shake hands.

Quinn reached up and shook Newman's hand. As he met the friendly look of the blue eyes, he nodded and said, "Likewise." When the handshake was over he turned, put the toe of his boot into the stirrup, swung aboard, and fell in alongside his new acquaintance.

As they rode along, Quinn took in impressions of Newman without having to stare at him. The man was probably about the same age as Quinn—not yet thirty, but old enough to have been in a few places. He had smooth, plain features and a suntanned face that, along with the light brown hair and sparkling blue eyes, gave him an easygoing appearance. He did not look as if he had been seasoned by the Wyoming sun and wind. After a man had been in the country awhile, he began to take on a color or tone that blended in with the rest of the world. Newman looked at home in the saddle, leading a horse, but it seemed as if he came from somewhere else.

As Quinn gathered impressions of the man's accent and manner as well as his appearance, he sensed a resemblance to other riders from the south. Quinn would not have said there was a single southern look, though, for he had also known the dark-featured, hatchet-faced, close-eyed, whip-jawed riders as well as the jowly teamsters with wet lower lips, all of whom claimed Texas, Arkansas, Louisiana, or Missouri as "back home." For the time being, it was enough to know that Newman had "come up through Cheyenne."

As Quinn rode on and took a glance now and then, he noticed that Newman kept an eye on his own backtrail, glancing over his shoulder from time to time. The man had a tan-colored, blanket-lined canvas coat tied to the back of his saddle, and sometimes when he turned in the saddle he felt for the coat with his right hand. For all his casual mannerisms, such as yawning or closing his eyes or tipping his hat down to his eyebrows, he reminded Quinn of men who habitually looked at a watch or felt for a wallet.

After the two of them had ridden for quite a while without talking, Newman spoke up. "I'll tell ya," he said, "I wish I'd rolled me a cigarette when we was stopped back there. I haven't had a smoke since I got my hands on this horse."

"Fine by me. I'll hold 'im for you." Quinn

stopped his horse and waited while Newman circled in back of the packhorse, came up on Quinn's left, and handed him the reins of the spare horse. Quinn nodded and sat holding the reins in one hand and the lead rope in the other.

Newman tucked his gloves under his leg, pulled the makin's out of his shirt pocket, and built a smoke. As he blew out the first cloud of smoke he nodded to Quinn and reached under the horse's jaw. "Thanks," he said as he took the reins back. He put on his gloves as he crossed in front of Quinn, and the two riders resumed their pace together.

Newman smoked the cigarette down to a flat little snipe and then pinched it dead with the gloved thumb and first two fingers of his left hand. He seemed ready for conversation again, for he looked across at Quinn and asked, "Where did you say you were workin' up in the Powder River country?"

Quinn ran his tongue across his lips. "I didn't say, but it was the Six Pines Ranch, run by a man named Bill Blackburn."

"Never heard of it," said Newman, shaking his head.

"Well, I never heard of the Lockhart Ranch before today."

Newman laughed. "It's a big country. Even a good-size ranch is just a dot on the map."

"That's right," Quinn agreed. "And there's a lot more small ranches than there used to be."

Quinn thought Newman was friendly without being too forward. In the general code of the country, a man didn't ask personal questions of strangers, but a question about work wasn't quite as personal as one about where a man came from or what he had done earlier in life. Naturally Quinn wondered about Newman, and after a few minutes he thought of a way to phrase his question.

"Have you been at the Lockhart Ranch for long?"

"Not so long," answered Newman. "Sully put me on in the spring, when all the work started up around here."

"Uh-huh." Quinn knew that most ranches hired a crew in the spring for roundup, kept the men through haying and fence building and fall roundup, and then let them go before winter set in. A small ranch would keep on only a man or two through the winter. If Newman had just hired on this spring and had come up through Cheyenne only "a while back," as he had said, it was probably his first season in Wyoming. That checked with the general impression Quinn had already formed.

"It's not bad," Newman went on. "Sully pays his men every month, which is better'n I can say for some, and the grub is edible."

"How is he for a boss?"

"Not so bad, as far as bosses go. He's a little dry."

"Oh? How's that?"

"He's pretty stuck on work. Especially on roundup, you put in long days and don't sleep much. Sully, he eats standin' up. He doesn't push us as much right now with roundup over, but he's still not a barrel of fun."

"Uh-huh."

"There's no liquor allowed on the ranch, and that's that. You save your jokes an' women talk for when he's not around."

"Is he fair?"

Newman raised his eyebrows and tipped his head. "Oh, yeh. He's got no favorites, and he does his share of the work. He's not afraid to get wet, cold, or dirty."

"I mean, is he square with each of his hands, man to man?"

Newman gave Quinn a sidelong look and then said, "Oh, yeh. I'd say so. He might not treat ya much better'n a Mexican, but you know how you stand with him."

Quinn looked back at his packhorse and then at Newman. "Sounds like someone I could work for," he said. "That's about all you can expect—fair wages, decent grub, and square treatment."

"Isn't that the truth," declared Newman. "And it's a hell of a lot more'n you git in a lot of places."

Quinn answered, "It sure is." He realized he felt at ease with the other man. Newman worked for wages like he did, and he had the comrade spirit. Quinn felt a twinge of guilt as he imagined Newman kept an unanswered question to himself. It would be reasonable for Newman to wonder why a cowhand like Quinn, who was not new to the country, was looking for work in the middle of the season. Quinn imagined he would get around to telling the story if he stayed for any while at all. From the sounds of it, he thought it would be all right if this Sully Lockhart had a place for him at the bunkhouse.

Chapter Two

Quinn had played the episode back and forth in his mind a thousand times, to the point that it had gotten distilled. Now, whenever he recalled the experience, it seemed as if it came up from his stomach, all wormwood and bitters.

The Six Pines Ranch, run by Bill Blackburn but owned by a board of investors in Chicago, had come into being in the aftermath of the Johnson County cattle wars. The cattle business was no longer in the control of a handful of huge outfits, and the country was giving way to more and more small, independent ranches. Still, there lingered the old prejudice that anyone who was a small operator was likely to be a mavericker and therefore a rustler.

A man like Bill Blackburn, who had always been a company man for one outfit or another and had never owned a head of beef himself, could talk out of both sides of his mouth. Out of one side came a defense for the new ranches, since the Six Pines was building itself up after having bought out a couple of smaller outfits. Then from the other side of his mouth came the company policy, which some of the punchers said Bill had instigated. Anyone who worked for the Six Pines Ranch could not have his own place or his own cattle. A man who had his own claim and his own brand was likely to put that brand on a maverick—or, worse yet, on an unbranded calf that was not a stray. As Blackburn explained it, that was a possibility the Six Pines Ranch would prefer not to deal with, and in order to remove the element of suspicion, the ranch had its simple rule.

Under Bill Blackburn's management, the rule seemed to perpetuate the element of suspicion rather than remove it. As Quinn saw it, the rule accused everyone in advance. But since he didn't have a place of his own, or a brand, or so much as a milk cow, he thought he could work at the Six Pines and not take the rule personally. That was before he understood Blackburn and his right-hand man, Cullen.

Cullen had been at the ranch for just one year ahead of Quinn, but in that first season, as the story went, he had worked himself into Blackburn's favor and had been kept on to draw winter wages. Cullen was a lean, quiet man with short blond hair flecked with white. The other hands said that when Cullen first came to the ranch he looked like a down-at-the-heel saddle tramp. He had tattered clothes, and his long hair had bits of hay and straw from the places where he had been sleeping. But after a while at the Six Pines he smartened up, and from then on he shaved every day except on roundup and kept his hair cropped above his ears.

Blackburn was the kind of man who had to be boss and who had to be sure his men knew he was the boss. Cullen, who was willing to carry out orders and to carry back information, was the type of man to serve Blackburn's purposes. Cullen was not above checking a man's saddle skirts to see if he carried a running iron, and he seemed to keep track of every puncher's string of horses. More than once he had told Quinn that Bill wanted him to work this horse or that one a little more.

Cullen also handed out the mail when any came through. Quinn always looked forward to a letter from Sarah, but when it came to him through Cullen's hand, as it invariably did, he felt it had been logged in Cullen's invisible ledger.

For the most part, Quinn managed to ignore Cullen's manner. All through spring roundup he went about his job, followed orders, and minded his own business. He rode his own string, taking the rank horses with the gentle ones. At the branding he roped when it was his turn, just as he wrestled calves, ate dust, and took his kicks. When he went to the chuck wagon he felt he had earned his grub honestly, and wherever he rode beneath the endless sky, he felt beyond suspicion.

Blackburn usually sent the men out in pairs, as was the custom. He varied the assignments so that Cullen made the rounds, working every four or five days with each hired man. Perhaps two days out of five, Quinn worked with Morgan, a fellow cowpuncher who was an all-around good hand at riding and roping. Quinn got along with Morgan as well as he did with anyone, but the general atmosphere at the Six Pines did not lend itself to the making of close friends.

Then one day on roundup, Blackburn fired Morgan, right in front of the other punchers at midday chuck. He said he had learned that Morgan was partners with a man named Dukes, who had his own little homestead claim and was starting to run a few cows.

Morgan said it was true.

Blackburn said it was against the company's rules, since a partnership made a man half owner of outside stock. He told Morgan to pack his bedroll.

All this while, Cullen was standing by, and from the air of the proceedings, Quinn did not doubt that Cullen had had a hand in the matter.

When spring roundup was over, Quinn went into Buffalo with the rest of the boys. By then Sarah had gone back to Cheyenne, as her father had finished his land surveying in Johnson County. Being at liberty, Quinn went to the saloons with the other Six Pine riders.

Before long he ran into Morgan, who had some

cross things to say. He said he'd been as much as blacklisted. No one who was hiring would put him on, and he had heard the word was out that he was a mavericker.

Blacklisting wasn't as formal as it had been in the eighties and on up to the big trouble of '92, but word of mouth traveled among the ranchers who were big enough to hire a crew. Morgan said he was through in the Powder River country, and so was Dukes, since the two of them depended on Morgan's wages to get started and keep going. He said they were selling out and going on to Idaho.

Quinn said it was a rotten deal, and he didn't know the country was still that way.

Morgan said it wasn't as bad as it used to be, that it was getting better, but one man with shit in his neck could ruin another.

Quinn and Morgan had a few more drinks as they hashed through the topic. By then Cullen had come into the saloon, and Morgan glared at him. Then he said to Quinn, in a loud voice, "There's the ass-kisser now. It makes me sick to look at him. I'd better leave before I do something I wish I hadn't."

When Quinn got back to the ranch a couple of days later, Blackburn told him he could pack his gear. When Quinn asked why, Blackburn told him he didn't have enough work.

Quinn only said, "That's a poor way to run a ranch."

Blackburn answered, "You won't have to worry about me ever runnin' one for you, cowboy."

Quinn gathered up his own two horses, which

had been in the horse pasture all through roundup, and he left as he had come—riding one horse, leading another, and looking for work. Now he knew better than to look for it in the area around Buffalo. He could go back north to Montana, where he had worked before, or he could point his horse south and east, in the direction of Cheyenne.

As he rode south for the next several days, his bitterness settled in. Quinn had not said anything at the ranch when Morgan got fired, and he wouldn't have expected anyone to stick up for him in turn. At a place like the Six Pines, a man watched his own back. Quinn knew that at one time he would have shrugged off the incident, telling himself he didn't want to work for an outfit like that anyway. But a few years did something to a man, made him take life more seriously. Having seen a repugnant side of human nature, Quinn couldn't just ignore it. He had been in the midst of an injustice he resented—more on Morgan's behalf than on his own—and now his stomach tightened at the thought of what some men would do in the name of a job.

The code of the country, at least among the working men, was based on trust. Until he knew otherwise, a man assumed he could trust the men he rode with. It didn't matter where another fellow had been before, or what he had done; if he rode for the same brand, you assumed you could trust him. Blackburn had shown no respect for that basic trust, and Cullen had outright sold it out. It had been an ugly episode to live through and be part of, and Quinn felt that something had been lost. He wondered if he would find it again.

"He's a good 'un," said Newman.

Quinn looked up and followed the motion of Newman's tilting head. A couple of hundred yards off to the right, bright as he stood in the sunlight against a pale grassy hillock, stood a buck antelope. The animal stood in profile, with its white-and-tan body topped by a stately head and a set of thick black horns.

"You eat 'em?" asked Quinn.

"Not much. But there's rich boys that like to shoot 'em. It's good to remember where we seen this fella."

They rode onward, veering now to the southwest. The rolling grassland gave way to broken country, in some places dry and sere but in others graced by small green washes and watercourses. Newman was taking them toward a spot where dark treetops showed above the folds of the rangeland.

Another half mile brought them into a sheltered basin with a fringe of cedar trees on the west rim. Downslope from the cedars, the ranch headquarters lay spread out. From the positioning of the ranch itself as well as of the various buildings, Quinn imagined the strongest winds came from the west and northwest. The buildings were laid out in three sections—a long, low barn on the left, then a typical homestead house with a pyramid-shaped roof, and then on the right flank another long, low building that Quinn assumed was the bunkhouse and cook-shack. The barn and the bunkhouse each lay at an angle to the ranch house, so that the buildings together formed a stiff-jointed curve to follow the shape of the land that rose behind the buildings.

Quinn supposed the Lockhart Ranch had been in existence for a few years at least, as the lumber was all bleached and grayed from the climate. There were no frills, but it wasn't a rawhide outfit, either. The place was neat and snug and kept up.

In the center of the ranch yard stood a cottonwood, not tall but obviously at its full growth, with rough bark and a couple of jagged wounds where branches had broken off. Beneath the tree sat a four-wheeled ranch wagon—perhaps the wagon that had brought in the injured kid.

The shadows were beginning to reach out across the yard, but except for a thin wisp of smoke rising from a stovepipe in the bunkhouse roof, nothing stirred. Quinn figured the other men were still out at work. As the horses moved farther into the yard, the front door of the ranch house opened, and a man stepped out onto the shaded porch.

"That's the boss," said Newman in a low voice, as he moved his horse toward the house.

Quinn followed, letting Newman take the lead.

"How's the kid?" Newman called out.

"Looks like he broke a leg," came the voice. "I sent Dexter to bring back a doctor if he could."

"Uh-huh."

"At least you brought back the horse and saddle."

"That I did. Took a while, but I got him." Newman turned in his saddle to motion with his left hand. "This here is Quinn. Say's he's passin' through and lookin' for work. Seems like a good hand."

Quinn felt himself wince at the compliment.

"Might be," came the voice. The man stepped forward and said, "I'm Sully Lockhart."

Quinn took a look at the owner of the Lockhart Ranch. He was a thin man of about average height, about forty years old. At the moment he was hatless, having just stepped out onto the porch. He had dark hair, still in good supply on top but not coming down very far on the forehead. He had brown eyes set wide apart, with thin eyebrows and high cheekbones. His nose seemed to have a dent on the left side of the bridge, which was common in a world of right-handed men but may have been with him since birth, as it was smooth as a baby's spoon.

"Pleased to meet you," said Quinn.

"The same here." The wide-set eyes moved from Quinn to the packhorse. "You can go ahead and turn your horses into the corral. Hang your hat in the bunkhouse for the night, at least. I don't know yet if I need to put on another hand, but I'll let you know."

"Obliged," said Quinn.

27

"Thanks, Sully," Newman added.

"Don't mention it," said the boss, who then turned and walked back into the house.

Newman led the way into the barn, where he and Quinn stripped the horses, brushed them down, and turned them into a pole corral. Quinn offered to fork the hay into the hayrack, so Newman stood by and rolled a cigarette. He was halfway through smoking it when Quinn was done with the little chore of pitching hay.

"Well," said Newman, raising his eyebrows as he took a drag on the cigarette, "shall we go look in on Dudley?"

The kid from back east was lying on his bunk with a pained scowl on his face. He was long and pasty-looking as he lay in his undershirt and trousers, showing bare arms and bare feet. His hands were clasped behind his head, and his elbows stuck out. He had dark wavy hair and beady blue eyes, and his mouth lay open even when he wasn't talking. After Newman had introduced Quinn, the kid said, "I think it's broke. In fact, I know it is. I'm all done makin' wages this summer, and it's all because of that horse. I know it." He looked at Quinn, and with the same air of resentment he said, "You'll probably get my job, and welcome to it. I wouldn't care if you rode that horse plumb into the ground."

"Cheer up, Dudley," said Newman. "Life hasn't come to an end yet. Why, hell, I've known men with gangrene that couldn't git to a doctor. Now, *they* were in trouble. And here you are, with all

the comforts of home—except maybe a pretty girl
to rub liniment on you, of course."

"Thanks," said Dudley, who closed his mouth
and turned his scowl toward the floor.

Newman showed Quinn to the washbasins,
where the two men cleaned up.

"Kid's takin' it hard," said Newman, "but I
think everything'll work out all right."

When the two of them were cleaned up, they
took homemade chairs from the bunkhouse and
sat outside in the shade of the building. After a
while, a cowpuncher in a dark hat came riding
into the yard on a chestnut horse. He waved and
then took his horse into the barn. About fifteen
minutes later he came out of the barn and
crossed over to the bunkhouse. He was well-built
and dark-haired, probably in his early twenties.
He was wearing a dark hat with the brim turned
up on the sides and troughed in front and back.
His head seemed to bob up and down, and he had
a smile on his face.

"Hello, Newman."

"Afternoon, Jeff."

"Thought this was Jimmy at first, till I seen the
beard."

"No, Sully says he went for the doctor."

"That he did."

"Then I wouldn't look for him until sometime
in the night."

" 'Magine you're right." Jeff pinched his nostrils
with the thumb and forefinger of his right hand.
Then he wiped his hands on his sleeves, intro-

duced himself as Jeff Sipe, shook Quinn's hand, and went into the bunkhouse.

"We ought to hear the supper bell before long," Newman said. He leaned his chair back, drew out the makin's, and rolled himself a cigarette.

Before Newman had finished the cigarette, a rider on a gray horse came down the road into the basin. Quinn thought it might be the puncher who had gone for the doctor, but he heard Newman say, "Looks like we got more company."

Quinn watched as the horse and rider came in. The man was husky and blond, and probably younger than Quinn. He wore a full mustache, which looked white as the evening sun struck it. Closer now, he had the look of a grub line rider, with a warbag tied on behind his saddle. He rode over to the bunkhouse and looked down at Quinn and Newman.

"Light and set," said Newman, in a cheerful tone.

"Thanks. I think I will." The rider swung down and tied his horse to the hitching rail, then beat dust off his gray shirtsleeves and brown vest. He wore a round, short-brimmed, dark brown hat with four pinches in the crown to form a peak. Quinn expected him to dust the hat, too, but he just pushed it back on his head a ways.

"Is the boss around?" asked the stranger.

Newman motioned with his head. "Might be in the big house."

Quinn almost laughed, since the ranch house was anything but big.

"Do you know if he's hiring?" The stranger still loomed above the two men sitting against the building.

"Sure don't," said Newman, putting the cigarette to his mouth. "He don't let us know things like that."

"Uh-huh." The man turned to his horse and loosened both the cinches—looser than Quinn liked to see, but it was none of his business, he told himself. The husky man turned around. "Name's Cater."

"Mighty fine," answered Newman. "This is Quinn, and I'm Newman."

Cater nodded. "And the boss is Lockhart, isn't he?"

"Yessir," Newman answered. As Cater made a half-turn in the direction of the ranch house, Newman stuck the tip of his tongue out of the right corner of his mouth, then said, "He'll probably come on over as soon as the supper bell sounds. Make yourself at home."

Cater turned back and looked at Newman. The man had displeasure in his blue eyes. He had no doubt expected an invitation, which was to be expected in cow country, but he apparently didn't care for Newman's offhand manner. He tipped his chin and raised his eyebrows, as if in question.

"Go on in," said Newman. "You'll find Sipe and Dudley in there."

At that moment the door of the cookshack opened, and a pale arm reached out to beat the triangle. Quinn imagined the arm belonged to the cook, who had been banging around in the kitchen when Quinn and Newman had been washing up.

Newman settled his chair forward onto all four legs, dropped the stub of his cigarette into the dirt, and put the sole of his boot onto it. He looked at Quinn and said, "Callin' our name."

Sully came into the bunkhouse wearing a dark brown hat with a narrow ridge in the crown. He hung it on a peg next to the other hats, and Quinn noticed it had a black horsehair hatband.

Sully made Cater's acquaintance with the same reserve he had shown Quinn, and supper got under way without ceremony. As Newman had mentioned earlier, the conversation around Sully was none too lively. The boss did take his meal sitting down, but he ate quietly and left as soon as he had downed his coffee.

Quinn ate his own supper without speaking. No man had to feel uncomfortable about eating at another outfit's table or wagon, but he felt edgy at the idea that he and Cater were both at the ranch with the same purpose. He expected that come morning, at least one of them would be moving on.

When Sully was gone and the tableware had all gone to the kitchen, Newman and Sipe brought out their smoking materials. Newman rolled a smoke as always, and Sipe stuffed tobacco into a reddish-brown pipe with a curved stem. Before long a cloud of tobacco smoke hovered over the table, and Cater coughed. Then he got up and walked out the back door.

Sipe seemed to be the sort who was always in a good humor, with his eyes sparkling and at least a half-smile on his face. He looked at Quinn and said, "There's lots of interestin' things to be seen out here."

Quinn nodded. "I imagine."

"I mean real interestin'. There's bones of animals ten times bigger'n any animal you ever seen."

"Uh-huh."

"An' then there's the Indian caves."

"Really?"

"Yeh, up in the mountains. I'd like to go git a better look at 'em someday. I've got a hunch some of 'em belonged to some of them drorf Indians that they talk about."

"Dwarfs?"

"Yeh. Little bitty Indians. Who knows how long ago. They say all the old Indian legends talk about the Little People, especially north and west of here. They hid in the mountains, and like as not, there's caves that has some of their remains. Maybe little caves, that reg'lar Injuns couldn't get into. Tremendous things, that ord'nary people don't get to know about."

Quinn was about to utter an expression of agreement when a noise came through the open door from the hitching rail outside. He heard the grunts of a thrashing horse, and then a loud squeal.

All three of them—Quinn, Newman, and Sipe—were up with a scraping of the chairs as they pushed away from the table. Newman was out the door first, followed by Quinn, who saw the problem at a glance.

Cater's horse was lying on its right side, flailing and kicking in the dust. Apparently the saddle had slipped around to hang upside down on the underside, and the horse had tried to kick it off. Now it had its left hind foot caught in the gear, and it was giving powerful lurches as it rocked back and forth. It had broken the reins from the hitching rail, and it lifted its head twisting up into the air.

Quinn thought it took some nerve to do what Newman did. The man stepped into the middle of the commotion, with his jackknife already open. The saddle was upside down, with its off side facing Newman. He jerked the front cinch and unbuckled it, then slashed the rear cinch strap with his knife. The hind leg kicked free, and the big gray horse came up, head and front feet first, as the saddle fell to the ground. Newman dropped his knife and grabbed the short reins, then bore his weight down to keep the horse's head from jerking back. After a few more seconds of pawing and digging backward the horse came to a standstill, shivering as it heaved through its widened nostrils.

"Someone give me a hand," said Newman.

"I will." Cater's voice came from the doorway. The big man stepped down into the dust, where his saddle and warbag lay ground into the dirt and fresh manure. He untied a rope from his saddle, moved to the horse's neck, slipped the rope around it, and tied a quick bowline knot.

Newman let go of the reins and backed away.

Cater played out some slack and let the horse relax. He gave a pained looked at his broken reins and then his mangled tack. "Ruined my outfit," he said.

"He did raise hell with it," said Newman.

Cater glared at Newman. "I mean you. You cut my cinch."

"Sorry," Newman answered. "But he was in a tight spot."

"If you'd waited another second and kept your hands off my gear, I'd've taken care of it."

Newman picked up his knife and put it away. Then he took a deep breath, dropped his shoulders, and said, "If you wouldn't've left him tied up that way, with the cinches all loose, it wouldn't have happened to begin with." After a pause he said, "I'd think you might thank me instead of gettin' het up about it."

Cater's blue eyes continued to blaze at Newman, and the spit jumped from his mouth as he said, "I'll thank you to keep your hands off my horse and gear, that's what."

Newman shrugged.

Cater took a couple of steps toward his saddle, picked it up and gave it a shake, and set it back down. He looked at Newman. "You've been smart with me ever since I first rode up."

Quinn became aware of Sully standing on the dark porch of the ranch house.

"Look," said Newman. "Maybe it doesn't take that much to get you riled. But if it'll make you happy, I'll apologize for cuttin' your cinch. Me 'n' Sipe can mend that and your reins both in the time it takes you to straighten out the rest of your outfit."

Newman looked at Sipe, who nodded and grinned and said, "No harm done."

By the time darkness fell, Cater had his horse put away and his gear all put together. The men were all back in the bunkhouse, joined now by the cook, who was a little dark-haired man named Moose.

Cater was still surly, but he had apparently cooled off and remembered he was looking for work. For a while he sat quietly, with his large pale mustache moving up and down as he chewed tobacco. Eventually he fell into the general line of talk, and in the course of conversation it came out that he had just come to Wyoming. He said he had helped bring a horse herd from eastern Nebraska to the Cheyenne River country and from there had come south looking for work.

Then it was Quinn's turn to account for himself. He stated briefly that he had been up in the Powder River country.

"I heard they'd had a little trouble up there," Cater interjected. "Heard they had to turn some fellows loose from a place called the Six Pines Ranch."

Quinn looked at Newman and then around at the other faces in the room. "That's where I was working," he said. He knew that Cater couldn't say any more without calling him a rustler, on the basis of hearsay, so he let the silence hang in the air.

"That's an idea," said Newman, smiling at Cater. "If they let some men go, they're probably lookin' for a good hand."

Cater looked sideways at Newman, then twitched his big mustache as he sniffed. "I don't know if that's the kind of place I want to work at."

Dexter came in with the doctor in the middle of the night. The doctor took a look at the boy's leg and said he should take him back to Lusk in the morning. Then the lights went out, and Quinn listened to the other men fall asleep until he, too, drifted back to the land of tangled dreams.

When gray light was filtering into the bunkhouse, Quinn heard the other hands getting up. He pulled his clothes on and went out with Sipe to hitch up the doctor's horses. Sipe was cheerful as before, but Quinn couldn't tell if there was just a touch of hesitation in the man's manner. If there was, Quinn thought, it might be based on Cater's remark about the Six Pines Ranch.

Newman and Sipe and Dexter all had their horses saddled and ready before breakfast. Quinn understood that Sully gave his orders at breakfast, and everyone rode out from there.

Sully ate his breakfast and fried potatoes, drank down his coffee as he stood up, and put on his dark hat with the horsehair hatband. He told Sipe and Dexter to help the doctor and the kid get on their way. Then he turned to the other men.

"Quinn," he said, looking at him with the wide-set eyes, "go ahead and saddle a horse out of Dudley's string. Newman can tell you which one. Then you can ride out with him and finish the job they started yesterday."

Cater had just cut a chew of tobacco off of a plug, and he was wiping the blade of his knife on his trousers leg when Sully turned to him.

"Cater," the boss said, "I don't have any more work than that. I wish you luck."

Cater moved his mouth, shifting the tobacco, as he nodded.

"You're welcome to stay on and get rested up if you want," Sully added.

Cater pulled a nickel-plated watch out of his vest pocket, looked at it, and said, "Thanks all the same. But I might as well move along." He put on his hat with the peaked crown.

Sully nodded to Cater, then to Quinn and Newman, and walked out of the bunkhouse.

Newman and Quinn left after him and went to the horse corral. Newman pointed out a roan horse for Quinn, who roped it and led it out of the corral as Newman worked the gate. Newman rolled a cigarette and smoked it as Quinn brushed the horse and saddled it.

As the two of them rode away in the early-morning sunlight, Newman said, "Sully's got a way about him, hasn't he?"

"How do you mean?"

"He didn't come right out and say it, but this is your string of horses to work with now."

Quinn raised his eyebrows. He already knew he had a job again, but he hadn't put it in those terms. "I guess so," he said. He patted the roan horse's neck, then looked around at Newman and said, "Thanks."

Chapter Three

Quinn took a deep breath, drawing in the cool, still morning as he rode out from the ranch. Newman rode on his left and talked about the general lay of the land, the roundup the crew had recently finished, and the other outfits that shared the range with the Lockhart Ranch.

Quinn and Newman rode several miles west of the ranch headquarters with the purpose of observing the general condition of the range and of the Lockhart cattle. Because most of the range was open, Sully's cattle would be mixed here and there with other brands, and the punchers were to take notice of anything unusual on that score, too. On the far end of the ride they stopped for a rest, both men sitting on the ground. Newman rolled a cigarette without letting go of his horse's reins.

"This is good country," said Quinn, chewing on a stem of grass.

"Oh, yeh," agreed Newman, smoking his cigarette and looking out across the landscape. "Especially in summer."

"It's hard to tell what it would be like to live here year-round, year in and year out. Everywhere a fella goes, he wonders if that's where he'll end up settling down."

Newman nodded, then said, "Some of it, though, a fella knows he's just passin' through."

Quinn looked at him and met the blue eyes. "Are you just here for the season, then?"

Newman wrinkled his nose. "I like it here well enough, but I'm thinkin' I'd like to make my way out to Oregon. I need a stake of money to travel on, though, so I'm afraid I might not get out of here before winter."

Quinn nodded. "You could always go back south and around that way."

"Oh, yeh." Newman took another drag on his cigarette. "I'm in no hurry."

After they had rested for a quarter of an hour, the two men mounted up. At this point they would split up, Quinn to go north and Newman to go south, so that each of them might take a wide semi-circle on the way back to the ranch. The sun was high at midmorning when they parted company, and they expected to be back at the bunkhouse for midday dinner.

Quinn let the roan horse step out at its own pace. It was a good walker, and now that it was headed back to the home corral it did not loiter.

As he rode, alone now, Quinn felt better than he had felt in quite a while. The country stretched out and away endlessly in all directions. The blue sky was empty, and the air was light and pure.

The animals also gave Quinn a feeling of tranquillity. He saw cattle spread out here and there, but none in big bunches. Once he saw a herd of five horses that turned and ran, disappearing in less than a minute. He also saw antelope from time to time, running and cavorting, flashing their white rumps against the pale green background of the prairie.

He heard the tinkling call of the meadowlark, always a happy song. At one point, about halfway back to the ranch, he saw a large red-tailed hawk soar down within ten feet of the ground until it lifted back up into the air currents.

He also saw prairie dogs, a couple of long-eared jackrabbits, a waddling badger, and three grouse that whirred up and spooked the roan horse.

But not one person did he see on the ride back. The world was quiet and calm as nature went on its course undisturbed, and Quinn felt the peace of the open country.

After the midday meal, the bunkhouse hands sat around for a short while. Dexter and Newman rolled cigarettes while Sipe loaded his pipe. Dexter, who had not seen much of Cater during the man's overnight visit, was interested in knowing the story about the traveler.

"So what about that blond feller?" he asked.

Sipe raised his eyebrows and had his usual

half-smile on his face as he poked his right index finger into the bowl of his pipe. "Said his name was Cater."

"Probably was," Newman commented. Then he added, "I believe he said he come from eastern Nebraska."

"Probably did," said Sipe, bobbing his head and tucking out the corners of his mouth.

The other punchers smiled along with him.

Dexter licked the edge of his cigarette paper and said, "Didn't seem like a real happy sort, from what I saw."

Sipe answered. "He had a gunbelt in his warbag. The tie-down kind. But I bet he's the type that would carry a little pistol in his boot along with it. I don't think he wants to get along."

Newman tapped the ends of his cigarette and then put it in his mouth. Before lighting it he said, "You can tell he's new to this part of the country and isn't sure how to go about it—plus bein' a sorehead."

Sipe blew out a rich cloud of smoke. "Why do you think he came out here?"

Newman squinted as he lit his cigarette. "Oh, he probably got tired of stackin' wheat and feedin' hogs, and thought he'd come out here where the livin's so easy."

Dexter shook his head once as he exhaled. "Not everyone is cut out for shortgrass country. You've got to take this country on its own terms—the way it is, and the way people are. Me, I come from that tallgrass prairie north of Lincoln, probably close to where this Cater come from, and I

like this country fine. But it takes some gettin'
used to. It's a different country. For one, it's drier.
But it's also just spread out more, in all kinds of
ways. You don't get ever'thing all at once. Like
Dudley needin' the doctor. Sometimes you just
have to wait for things to come around."

Sipe compressed his mouth as if he was on the
verge of a joke. "You two fellas bein' from the
same place, you don't act like it."

Dexter paused with his cigarette halfway to his
mouth. "What do you mean?"

Sipe ran his tongue across his lips. "You take
two horses that come from the same place, even
if they've never known each other before, and
they'll take right up to one another. It's a fact. I've
got two horses in my string that both come from
Castle Butte, and they're best friends. Sully says
he knows them two horses never knew each other
before. And I've heard the same thing in other
places, too."

"So have I," said Newman. "A horse might not
know his own brother, but he knows when they
come from the same place. I believe it."

Sipe bobbed his head. "Well, Jimmy, didn't you
feel no kinship with that feller?"

Dexter pursed his lips and then said, "Can't say
that I did. I think, with horses, they have to com-
municate it to one another. I didn't have much
palaver with this fella."

Sipe clicked the stem of his pipe against his
teeth. "You two are probably about the same age,
too."

Dexter, who had mentioned earlier that he had just turned twenty-eight on the Fourth of July, shook his head and said, "I didn't pick up any sense of kinship. He's a different breed of pup, was all I felt."

Sipe took in a long breath and let it out. He turned toward Newman and said, "He was a pretty jumpy customer. I thought maybe we were gonna see the feathers fly."

Newman yawned. "Oh, no. Not with me. I'd rather be able to laugh about it later."

Sipe laughed. "Yeh, his saddle sure took a roll in the manure, didn't it?" He looked at Quinn, who had been silent. "What do you think, Quinn?"

"I think he could've been trouble. I'm glad Newman played it with the soft touch."

In the afternoon, with a change of horses, Quinn and Newman rode north a few miles in the general direction of Lost Spring. At the far end of their ride they split up as before. This time Quinn hooked around to the left while Newman took off to the right. Just before they said so long, they looked at the clouds gathering in the west.

"Might get wet," said Newman, reaching back and touching the canvas jacket. "I wish I had a slicker."

"I've got one," said Quinn, "but it's not doin' me much good in the bunkhouse. I'll get it back into my routine by tomorrow, though." He looked at the sky. "Kinda like closing the corral gate after the horse got out."

45

The riders split up then, and after a few minutes Quinn looked behind him and saw only rangeland. It was as if the land had swallowed up the other rider and Quinn was the only person for miles. He continued on his ride, keeping an eye on the clouds as he made his sweep of the country. The clouds were starting to close in, and he could no longer see the mountains in the west. He decided that regardless of whether he got wet he wasn't going to hurry his work. Even if he pushed it, he could end up getting wet anyway, and he wanted to do the job he was sent out to do.

The country he rode through was similar to the range he had seen on his return ride before dinner, which was reasonable, as his return this afternoon would take him close to where he had been in the morning. Generally, the range that lay north of the ranch was rolling grassland, while the land to the south was a little poorer, with more broken country. The grass was in good shape this year, and the weather must have been encouraging, for Quinn passed two quarter-section homestead claims that were being turned over for wheat. In each, a crop of wheat was planted and more land was being worked.

He winced at the sight of the ripped-up ground. Just about anyone would like fried chicken, fresh eggs, garden vegetables, and farmers' daughters, but few cowmen—ranchers or cowhands—liked to see rangeland being plowed under. It meant just one more piece of the free country was lost. There was no way of fighting it, though. It was like the railroads, or the ditch projects, or anything else they called Progress. If enough people with political power wanted it, it was going to happen.

Quinn felt a bitter smile come to his face. What some people thought was progress could ruin the land. It was well known that not too long ago in the past, a little over twenty years, there hadn't been such a thing as a tumbleweed. The first tumbleweeds in this country grew in a wheat field, and now they were all over. They grew anywhere the original grass was disturbed, but they thrived best in abandoned wheat and cornfields where hopeful farmers had broken up the land, gone broke, and moved on to try their luck elsewhere. To protect their crops, the grangers had to fence out the cattle; then the fences did a good job of collecting tumbleweeds.

Not long after he saw the second piece of worked ground, Quinn topped a rise and saw a ranch house down on his right. Like others in this country it was a small, square building with a pyramid-shaped roof of wood shingles, which gave a dull shine in the darkening afternoon. Like the Lockhart layout, the house and its few additional small buildings sat up against a little ridge to the west.

Quinn decided not to go out of his way to make a large detour, so he rode straight down into the swale, cutting across at about a quarter of a mile in front of the house. He glanced in the direction of the house a couple of times but saw no activity; then, when he was past the house, a bright movement caught his eye. Looking again, he saw a woman on the south side of the house. She was taking clothes down from a clothesline. From the distance Quinn could not see much detail—just a light green dress and a head of long, dark hair— but the woman did not look old or frowsy.

Quinn glanced at the trail ahead and then back at the woman. As he did, she turned, and with her left arm full of clothes she raised her right hand and waved. Quinn felt a spark inside as he raised his right hand and waved back. Then his horse picked up its pace to go uphill, and he looked ahead. He wanted to look back again, but he knew it would seem deliberate. The woman was probably somebody's wife, and it would not do to be seen gawking at her.

It was a good thing the woman had taken in her laundry, he thought. The first few drops of rain were starting to fall. He heard them on his hat brim, then on the saddle leather, the horse, and the grass. He felt them on his hands—cool spots on his warm, dry skin. The drops came heavier now, and the air felt damp and cool, moving in a slight breeze that brought the smell of fresh rain on dust, grass, and horsehair.

Quinn rode on, keeping an eye on the clouds. They were not dark or heavy-looking, and they were moving overhead toward the east. Off to the southwest, where the clouds were thicker, he saw a flash of lightning. Nearly half a minute later, he heard a faint rumble of thunder.

Now the rain was dampening his shirt. He could feel the coolness on his arms and back. He looked again at the sky and felt the raindrops on his face. It looked as if it was going to be a gentle rain, coming down softly all around him as he rode alone on the spreading plain.

If it turned ugly, he thought, he would ride for a low spot. If it turned violent, he could ride hell-for-leather for that ranch house a mile back. There didn't seem to be a need for anything like that, though. The rain kept coming down, but it was not intensifying.

Quinn rode on for about a mile in the rain, thinking of the good it was doing for the range grass, the hay fields, and even the wheat fields. A slow, steady rain was better than a gully-washer, and every little bit helped here on the high plains, where things dried out so quickly. Even though he and his saddle were getting wet, he felt as if the world was right, with life going on and the rain drumming softly on the land all around him.

Eventually the clouds overhead broke up and moved to the east, where they seemed to gather again beyond the low hills. Now the sun came through the open sky to the west, and the rain faded away. Quinn heard the fluting song of the meadowlark, always a lovely sound in the fresh, clean air after a rain.

He glanced again at the clouds in the east, and he saw a rainbow. Its bright colors stood out against the background of leaden clouds.

A few minutes later he looked again at the rainbow, and this time he saw a double rainbow. The outer rainbow was not as dark as the first one. The inner rainbow had sharp colors, beginning with purple on the innermost band and then changing through blue, green, yellow, orange, and red. The outer rainbow, in addition to being fainter, had its colors in the opposite order. It began with red on its innermost band and then moved through the colors to end with a light purple on the outermost band. Quinn wondered if the second rainbow was a reflection of the first one.

It was an inspiring sight, this spontaneous display of color after a gentle rain, with the sunshine and the cool, damp air and the fresh-smelling grass and the silver tune of the meadowlark and nothing but the natural world for miles around. This was reverence, the way a cowboy felt it when he was one with creation.

Once before, when Quinn was working up in Montana, he had seen a double rainbow. He remembered the awe he had felt then, and he had thought of that feeling a few times in the meanwhile when life was not so good. It seemed as if that feeling had gone away, dried up, gotten lost. Now, with the fresh new world all around him, it seemed as if life could be good again, after all. He knew he would remember this moment, just as he remembered that earlier moment when, alone on the plain, he had seen the wonder of things beyond the reach of man.

Back at the bunkhouse, as the punchers were reporting what they had seen during the day, Quinn mentioned the double rainbow.

"Them's pretty," said Sipe, who was oiling the six-gun he had carried in his saddlebag.

Dexter was mending a pale blue shirt, a twin to the patched shirt he was wearing. With his dark head still bent over his work, he said, "Uh-huh."

Newman looked up from cleaning his fingernails with his pocketknife. "I wonder if a double rainbow means there's two pots of gold at the end," he said.

"I doubt it," said Dexter, who now looked up and showed his green eyes. "I doubt there's ever the first one."

Sipe held back the hammer of his pistol and twirled the cylinder. "It's a nice superstition," he said, "but I doubt it, too. I've been close enough to a rainbow to see exactly where the end touched down, and I've rode to the spot."

"How deep did you dig?" Newman asked.

"I knew better than to dig any at all," answered Sipe. "I could tell it was no different than any other place." He held the pistol close to his nose and sighted the gun at the far corner of the room. "It's a fact. I done it twice, and both times it was just grass and dirt, and no sign that anyone had ever buried anything."

"Hell," said Newman, "there's been dirt farmers have plowed up old Spanish swords from two, three feet under the grass—well, maybe two feet—and those things probably got buried by themselves. They've turned up old coins, too. You'd never know those things were there."

"If there's any of that kind of stuff, it's all farther south," said Dexter. "Main thing people dig up in this country is dead bodies."

"Now, that's a fact," said Sipe, laying the six-gun on the crate next to his bunk. "Down by Hartville—this was last year, just before winter, wasn't it, Jimmy?"

"Well, we were both still here at the ranch, so it must have been late October or early November."

"Anyway," Sipe went on, "there was a couple of kids diggin' a hole in the backyard, and they found some of them old blue bottles buried. The schoolteacher heard about it, and he said there was probably an outhouse there at one time, and people throw stuff like old bottles down the hole. He was interested in findin' some more of them old bottles, so him and the kids went back to diggin'. Only, instead of diggin' up more bottles they come to a man's head."

Newman smiled. "You don't say."

"Yep. Then they went and got the sheriff, and they dug around careful like, and they found where this fella had been buried sorter sittin' up."

"Then he didn't fall into the outhouse and die that way," said Newman, putting his knife away. "Or he'd been in there headfirst."

"No," said Sipe, "he didn't die that way. He had a bullet hole in his head."

Dexter clucked. "Been in there a good fifteen years, they figured. From the time of the first early copper mines, maybe."

"Those miners are a rough lot," said Newman.

"Oh, yeh," returned Sipe. "Them, an' railroaders, an' ditch graders."

"Uh-huh," said Newman. Then after a moment he asked, "Do they still mine copper there?"

Dexter shook his head. "Mostly iron now. It's still a rough town."

As Quinn was listening to all this talk, his thoughts went back to his afternoon ride on the prairies. He remembered the double rainbow, and then he remembered the woman and the ranch house he had seen earlier. When the conversation came to a lull, he spoke up. "There was something else I saw this afternoon, which I thought I'd mention."

The other punchers looked at him, as if to invite him back into the conversation.

Quinn glanced at Newman and then at the others. "After Newman and I split up this afternoon, I hooked around to the west and came down through that country. I passed a couple of homesteads where they had put in wheat and were rippin' up to put in some more."

Dexter and Sipe nodded, and then Newman did likewise.

Quinn went on. "And then a ways south of that, I saw a little ranch, and there was a woman outside takin' in the laundry. I didn't get a close look at her, but she had long dark hair."

"Delevan," said Sipe.

Dexter smiled, and his green eyes sparkled. "I didn't know Newman was such a gentleman."

Quinn looked at Dexter and then Newman. "Why is that?"

Dexter smiled. "Most fellas would take that ride themselves. Sipe and I always have to flip a coin."

"What for?"

Sipe's voice came chirping up. "To see who gets to go that way. That was Marie Delevan you saw. In addition to bein' young an' pretty, she's a widder."

Chapter Four

Quinn opened his eyes after he had rinsed the soap away. The small mirror above the wash-basin did not allow him to see his whole face at once, but as mirrors went it was bigger than some. He could see one eye at a time, grayish green today, and he could see good-size portions of his dark beard. He had decided to shave the upper and lower edges of his beard, which he did once or twice a week. With some hot water from Moose's kitchen he washed his whole face first. Then with a bar of shaving soap he worked up a lather and spread it on his cheeks and on the underside of his jaws and throat.

He had originally let the beard grow when he was on a fall roundup in Montana. Then he kept it through the winter, and when summer came around again he found that it worked all right against mosquitoes and sunburn, just as it had done against the wind and cold. To himself he admitted that he liked the beard because it took some of the emphasis away from his nose. Quinn had a thin, curved nose, the type that some boys in school called a hawk nose or an eagle beak. He thought the beard put it into better proportion.

Sarah had not liked the beard as much as he did, and she had gotten him to agree that he would shave it off at least for a little while, when . . . well, when they were ready to be together all the time.

Sarah Dowling, blond and prim with baby blue eyes and a small pretty mouth, had smiled at Quinn the first time they saw each other on the board sidewalk in Buffalo. Her father was a land surveyor and had moved his family to Johnson County for a year. Sarah said that at first she had missed Cheyenne terribly, because the house there was so much warmer and she had a fire-place in her own room, and the house in Buffalo was so cold. Then finally her Papa had ordered a wood-burning stove for her room in the new frame house, and she used the stove until the warm weather came. All through the summer, she said, it was a comfort to know that the stove would be there again in the fall. When she met Quinn at the end of the winter she said that she rather liked the cold weather and that when she had her own house and wouldn't have the hired girl Bella to tend the fire—well, then she would learn to do it herself.

Quinn told her there were boys in the world who would happily chop and fetch firewood, tend the fire, and shovel and haul ashes.

And she gave him the look that made his heart flutter, as her blue eyes softened and her delicate mouth pursed, before she said, "In Cheyenne we always had coal, and I think it gives off a better heat."

Quinn smiled and said, "There's boys that love to shovel coal to keep pretty girls warm and happy."

And he was right, and he could tell she knew it.

Afterward he would realize that his willingness to make her happy was the main reason she liked him. It made him feel good to know that he was one of the few people—like her Papa and her Mama, of course—who could make her happy.

By the time he was ready to go on roundup, he had kissed her a few times and they had talked about . . . well, a time when they would always be together. Of course, she was going to have to go back to Cheyenne with her Papa, and of course Quinn was going to have to decide what kind of work he was going to go into, but then they were going to be happy.

That was how things stood when Quinn went to work at the Six Pines. During roundup he received a letter from her in nearly every mail bag, and he answered every one. Her letters were full of the sweet sadness that seemed to fill her life, and on every page she told him how much she missed him. He assured her in his letters that he missed her more than ever.

Afterward he would realize that being apart kept them together, in their understated pledge, much better than if he had seen her every day. It was an old saying that absence made the heart grow fonder, and for as much as a man got tired of hearing the same old sayings, there was some truth to them. When her letters started arriving from Cheyenne instead of Buffalo, his heart did not grow any less fond.

When things went bad at the Six Pines Ranch and he found himself back on the trail, he wrote Sarah and told her he would be in Cheyenne as soon as he could get there, but probably not until after fall roundup. By then, he thought, she would have her cozy coal fire going again.

Getting turned loose from the Six Pines had left him confused until the bitterness began to set in. After a couple of days of leading the packhorse down the trail, he had sorted out his feelings enough to realize he was in no hurry to get to Cheyenne. The image of Sarah did not make his heart flutter like before. He knew he should have been happy to leave the Six Pines and hit a lope south, but when he thought of Cheyenne he felt a sense of dread. Still, he kept heading in that general direction, for he had said he would.

In the bunkhouses and around the campfires he had heard stories that he imagined now were like his own. A man bought a horse and then wondered how in the hell he would ever get rid of it. A man signed on with a trail herd, then found out the boss was a lunatic and the cook was a drunk. Quinn had even had dreams like that—

dreams in which he had enlisted in the Army or ended up in a crowbar hotel. In the prison dreams, he knew he had done something he couldn't go back on; the act itself was not there, but the sense of having done it was clear.

As far as things went with Sarah, he was not in that deep. He had given his words in a couple of ways—that he would go to Cheyenne, and that he would like to make her happy. On the smaller point he had no qualms, but on the larger one he was beginning to wonder if he should try to get out.

The boys had said there was a new post office in Lost Spring, and Quinn's awareness of its presence just to the north gave him the feeling that he should write another letter. His hesitation came from not knowing what kind of a letter he wanted to write.

Quinn dipped his hand in the warm water, wiped his cheeks and neck clean of remaining suds, and moved his face around to check his work in the mirror. Then he took the basin to the back door of the bunkhouse and tossed the water.

In the morning, Quinn and Newman hitched a four-horse team to the wagon that sat beneath the cottonwood tree. With a few tools and camping supplies they set off to the southwest. Sully had told them to go the river, set up a work camp, and start cutting corral poles.

The ride took Quinn through country he had not yet seen. Like the other rangeland he had seen since he had been at the Lockhart Ranch, some of it was good rolling grassland and some of it was broken country. Even the breaks had some good pasture, especially in the bottoms.

At the river the men found a spot where the tent would be in shade most of the day, and they pitched camp. Quinn dug a fire pit and lined it with river rocks while Newman, whistling, unharnessed the horses and set them out to graze. There was still some working time left to the day, so the two men got out the bucksaw and axes and went to work.

For the first half hour Newman made no comments about the work, but Quinn could tell he didn't care for it. Some of the earlier cowboys, it was said, flat refused to work with an ax or a shovel or a pitchfork. If they couldn't do it from horseback, they went somewhere else where they could. Newman wasn't that way, but he lost some of his good humor when it came to swinging an ax. He wrinkled his nose, curled his lip, and occasionally gave a fierce swing after the ax bounced off a limb he was trimming from the center pole. Then he would lower the ax and let out a long breath.

"Thank God he doesn't want any big logs," he said at one point, resting the handle of the ax against his knee and pulling his gloves on tighter.

"It could be worse," said Quinn, smiling. "At least we don't have to cut cabin logs and shape 'em."

Newman gave him a cold look and a half-smile. "He wouldn't get much of that out of me. I don't have enough lumberjack in me."

"Neither do I," Quinn agreed. "But it doesn't

hurt to know how to do these things, in case a fella ever has his own place."

"That's true," Newman said. " 'Course, then you could pick your jobs."

"Yeh, but eventually you'd have to get around to all of 'em."

Newman's eyes widened and he tugged at his gloves again. "Workin' for someone else, though, it's different. Seems like a man like Sully, he wants to try you out. And then, if he's like the rest of 'em, whoever does a job the best gets to do it the most." He smiled as he nodded at the ax. "That's why you don't want to shine too much at this kind of work."

Quinn laughed. "You mean you don't want to be a tie-hack some day?"

Newman blew out a quick, heavy breath and shook his head. "I can't drink that much whiskey."

Quinn laughed again. "But you know," he said, "I think most fellows choose what they end up in. It's not like it was in the old days, when your old man signed you up to be a blacksmith's boy or a stonecutter's apprentice, and there you were."

"That's true. This here's America, and if you don't like what you're doin', you can just roll your blankets and move on down the trail."

A thought flashed in Quinn's mind; the comment reminded him that Newman was a light traveler. In the few days Quinn had known Newman, he had gathered that the man did not travel with a packhorse. Here in the north, most travelers carried their gear on a second horse.

Some men called it a bed horse, which was another indication of how much a man lived by the rules of the country. Since Newman traveled light, Quinn figured he did not intend to travel too long in this part of the country.

By the end of the day they had over a dozen poles cut and trimmed. Always mindful of the possibility of rain, they stashed the tools beneath the wagon. Newman stuck his gloves in his hip pocket and drew out the makin's.

"Not bad," he said. "Sully only wants a couple hunnerd, doesn't he?"

"That's all," said Quinn, wrinkling his nose. "And then a wagon load of short ones for the posts."

They built a campfire and brought out a Dutch oven and a skillet. They had brought a shoulder of beef wrapped in a bedroll, and while Newman unwrapped the meat and cut steaks for supper, Quinn went rummaging through the heap of cut branches. He found two young green limbs that were just right for pothooks, and he used the saw to cut them at about thirty inches. With his pocketknife he trimmed them up, then went back to the campfire.

"I suppose we should hang this meat each night and then wrap it up in the day," he said to Newman.

"I suppose so." Newman looked up and around. "That branch there would do as good as any." He set his knife down and said, "Let me get these steaks cooking, and then I'll get a rope."

Quinn stood by as Newman set the steaks sizzling in the skillet and then took a rope from the wagon, fingered the coils, and tossed the rope up and over the limb. Quinn lifted the chunk of beef and carried it over to the dangling end of the rope. Newman fitted a slipknot over the joint end of the bone and then grabbed the long part of the rope to pull up the slack.

"We'll swing 'er up like a horse thief," Quinn said.

Newman looked at him with his mouth drawn together and said, "Where I come from, sayin' just that much could get a man in trouble."

Quinn laughed. "Hell, Cater came within an ace of callin' me a mavericker, and we all slept like babies."

Newman pulled on the rope, and Quinn felt the weight lighten in his arms. He looked at Newman, who winked and said, "Come and pull me some slack. I want to tie it off, and this ain't no long rope."

Quinn laughed again. The long rope or the wide loop was what a rustler threw. The joke about a short rope was that a man had to ride fast to use it. "You ride fast?" he asked.

It was Newman's turn to laugh. "This ain't my rope," he said. "It's an extra one that Sully let that kid use."

Later, as the two of them sat on the ground eating steak and biscuits, Newman looked up at the rope and said, "You won't catch Sully usin' a rope like that on his own rig."

Quinn had noticed earlier that Sully carried a rawhide lariat, which was a high-quality item. "No," he said, "not somethin' ratty like that."

Newman paused as he cut off a corner of steak. "Moose says ol' Sully spends half a winter on one of them rawhide ropes, cuttin' and trimmmin' and stretchin' and braidin' and stretchin' again. Then when he's done he's got the purtiest forty-foot rope you'll ever see."

"Winter days are long," Quinn remarked.

Newman raised his eyebrows. "A man's got to have patience for that kind of work. That and horsehair."

Quinn nodded. "I saw his hatband, too."

Newman tossed a piece of gristle into the fire. "I hope I don't ever learn that kind of patience."

Quinn caught his meaning. Some men learned to braid horsehair in the penitentiary, such as the one down at Laramie, where days were long all year round. "Me neither," he said. "But I doubt Sully learned it the way some fellas do."

"Nah," said Newman. "He comes by it naturally."

After supper, as Newman sat smoking by the fire, Quinn dragged a couple of dry branches to the firelight so he could break up twigs and small pieces for the next day's kindling. Camp chores usually divided up pretty easily, especially with just two men. Newman had offered to tend the fire and do the cooking, so that left Quinn to gather firewood and haul water. As a rule, Quinn did not like someone poking in on his fire, so he tried not to interfere with someone else's. As he watched the fire burn down, though, he thought the fire pit could use some tidiness. Newman was good about tossing on new pieces, but he didn't seem to care about the unburned ends that lay around the fringe. After confirming with Newman that they weren't planning to put on any more wood, Quinn took a stick about two feet long and flipped the unburned pieces into the fire.

Quinn sat back and relaxed, drawing into himself in silence. The river was gurgling and lapping in the background, and it was a clear, bright night overhead. The smell of the wood smoke was reassuring, and the taste of beefsteak lingered in his mouth. There might be a better job than cutting corral poles, he thought, but life was good enough at the moment.

When the fire was burned down to coals and was beginning to ash over, the wail of a coyote rose on the still night air.

Newman raised his head. "That one's not too far away."

"He might smell the meat," Quinn remarked. "They can pick up a smell from quite a ways off."

"Let him whine," said Newman. "If he can jump that high, he can have it."

A little later on, as they were settling into their blankets, Quinn spoke up. "Where was it you come from, where people are so touchy about mentionin' horse thieves?" He figured he could ask, since Newman had brought it up.

Newman cleared his throat. "Horse country," he said. Then he laughed and rolled over. "Texas, Quinn. Down by Amarilla."

Quinn heard the coyote howl again, and when it subsided with a yap, he asked, "Do they have a lot of horse thieves there?"

"Not as many as they used to."

Quinn and Newman worked for several more days at cutting poles. On the second afternoon they got rained on and even had a few pea-size hailstones, so they had to spend a little while under the wagon. Then the storm passed, and the rest of the time they saw good weather.

Once he had settled into the rhythm of the work, Quinn found himself enjoying it. He liked the powerful feeling that came to his arms as he swung the double-bit ax, and it gave him pleasure to see the blade cut where he aimed it. The camp was near a good grove of cottonwoods, with plenty of young trees that were just right for corral poles. As he dragged out a freshly cut pole, Quinn admired the neat white spots where his ax had sheared the branches, and he took satisfaction in seeing the stack of poles grow.

Toward the end of their third day on the river, the men had a visit. A stranger came down into the river bottom on horseback and rode to the spot where Quinn and Newman were working. He was a large, burly-looking man in a broad-brimmed, drab gray hat that cast a shadow on his face.

"Music to my ears," he said, as he drew his horse to a stop.

Newman had rested his ax head on the ground,

and now he tilted the handle toward the visitor. "All yours," he said. "Have at it."

"Oh, no," said the stranger, looking down. "It's music when I hear someone else working."

"Good enough," said Newman, still smiling. "What can we do for you?"

"Not much," said the other man. "I was passin' by, and I saw your horses picketed up there, and then I heard this music, so I thought I'd come down and say hello."

"Glad you did," said Newman. "Gives me a reason to let my helper have a rest." He winked at Quinn, then turned back to the stranger. "This here's Quinn, and I'm Newman. We work for Sully Lockhart, and he's got us down here cuttin' corral poles."

"Well, I'm T. J. Blair." The man swung down from his saddle and stepped forward to shake Newman's hand. Then he shook Quinn's. "Pleased to meet both of you."

Quinn saw the man better now, although his face was still in partial shade from the broad brim of the hat. The man's forehead sloped straight down to an upturned nose without a break or ridge from the brow. He had a recessed chin so that the mouth looked tucked back beneath the upper lip, and his jowls looked as if they hadn't been shaved in nearly a week. He was a big man, taller than either Quinn or Newman, and barrel-chested. Quinn thought he looked a little like a badger.

"Passin' through?" Newman asked.

Quinn's glance flickered at the man's saddle, which had a coat of coarse gray wool tied behind the cantle. Then he looked back at Blair.

The man blinked and said, "No, I've got a place a little southeast of here, on Spring Creek."

"Oh," said Newman. "We're practically neighbors. I missed you during roundup. Are you a stockman?"

"My brand's the TJ," Blair answered. "Lou Stoller was reppin' my brand and a couple others."

"Oh, I remember that."

Blair went on. "So I run those cattle, and I trap, too. Lou was reppin' for me because I knew I wouldn't be back in time from sellin' my winter furs."

"Uh-huh." Newman nodded. "You hunt, too?"

The man blinked and smiled. "Been known to." He turned to Quinn and said, "Been workin' for Sully for very long?"

"Just this week."

"Well, this is good country," said Blair. "I'm glad to see Sully's makin' improvements." Then he added, quickly, "Hope he don't get too big, though," and he gave a quick laugh. He looked at the stack of poles and shook his head. "Lot of work," he said. "I've sat and marveled for hours at how beavers can do it." Then he laughed again. "Made me tired."

Quinn spoke. "Well, we're about done for the day anyway, aren't we, Newman?"

"Yeh, I think so." Newman turned to Blair and said, "You're welcome to set for a while."

"I think I will."

Quinn and Newman carried their tools back to the camp, and Blair followed leading his horse. He tied the horse to the front wheel of the wagon, away from the camp, and then sat on the ground with his new acquaintances. Newman brought out the makin's and offered the little cloth sack to Blair, who shook his head and pointed to his stubbled cheek, which was bulging.

"Just got a chew," he said, and turned aside to spit out a dark stream of tobacco juice.

Newman rolled a smoke with his usual neatness, popped a match, and lit up.

"I can see this ain't a Mormon camp," said Blair.

"Not by a hell of a lot," Newman answered. "Why do you mention it?"

"Well, I've got some snakebite medicine that might go down pretty good."

Newman looked at Quinn, who said, "Fine by me."

Blair pushed himself up and went to his horse. In another minute he was back with a pint flask wrapped in burlap. He pulled out the cork with a squeak and handed the bottle to Quinn.

The liquor smelled like regular whiskey, so Quinn tipped himself a little swig.

"Don't be shy," said Blair.

"That's fine for me," said Quinn. He handed the bottle to Newman, who rubbed his palm across the mouth of the bottle, as if by habit, and tipped a drink.

Blair took the bottle with outstretched arm, winking and blinking at his two comrades. "This ain't none of that two-bit tarantula juice, is it, boys?"

"No," said Quinn. "It's good-enough whiskey."

"Just like my mama used to make," said Newman.

The big man laughed and said, "Mine, too."

They sat for a while and made small talk about the country and the weather. Blair passed the bottle again, and Newman rolled another cigarette.

"What's a fella do around here in the winter if he doesn't trap?" Newman asked.

"Not much if he doesn't have a woman," Blair answered. "If you've got your own place and you put up hay, you prob'ly feed cows. That, and mend harness, and read catalogs." He blinked and looked at Newman. "You plannin' to stick out the winter?"

Newman held his cigarette sideways and looked at it. "I don't want to, but I think I need a little bigger stake than I'm gonna get on Sully's wages. I might could use a little more work at the end of the season."

"Oh."

"Just a thought." Newman took a drag.

"Hell," said Blair, turning to spit. "See about takin' out some greenhorns to do some huntin'."

Newman nodded. "I ain't done that before."

The big man laughed. "They don't know that." He turned to Quinn. "How about you? Are you stickin' out the winter, too?"

"I haven't thought that far ahead."

Blair scratched his recessed chin. "You're probably the smartest one of the bunch."

After a little more talk and another round with

the bottle, the shadows were stretching across the campsite. Quinn was thinking about offering to start the campfire when Blair said he had better be on his way. The big man pushed himself up onto his feet and brushed off the seat of his trousers.

"Don't be in a hurry," said Newman. "We've got grub enough for company."

"Thanks anyway," replied Blair. "But I've got a woman at home, and she'll have somethin' ready for me when I get back."

"Good enough," Newman said back.

"Glad you dropped in," Quinn added.

"So am I. Nice to meet you fellas." Blair tugged at the brim of the gray hat. "Drop by and see me anytime." Then he walked steadily to his horse, untied it, mounted up, and rode away.

When the man was several minutes gone, Quinn said, "Well, there's a neighbor to add to the list."

Newman, who had been whittling a toothpick, closed his pocketknife and put it away. Nodding at Quinn, he said, "He's all right."

Chapter Five

Quinn closed his left eye and sighted along the tops of the corral posts. "See if you can bring it down a little," he said.

Newman grasped the post with both gloved hands and pounded it into the hole three times. Then he steadied it for Quinn to have another look.

"Good enough," said Quinn. The cut white tops of the posts were nicely even. He walked back to where Newman stood holding the upright post. "Let's bury 'em," he said.

Quinn picked up the other post, set it into the other half of the hole, slammed it down a couple of times, and checked the top for level. Then he and Newman kicked in loose dirt from the mound and started tamping.

Sully's method for building a pole corral

entailed setting the posts in pairs and then running the poles between them. The poles overlapped where they met between the posts, so the men did not have to measure and cut the ends. Occasionally they had to trim an end to fit between the posts, but otherwise the laying of the poles went along without much delay. Setting the posts demanded more time and labor.

Quinn took a deep breath and exhaled as he continued to tamp with the shovel handle. Sully had let them work on through Sunday and had sent them no relief. Quinn and Newman had cut all the poles and posts, peeled them, and then spent three days hauling them to the ranch. Work was work, though, and Quinn liked the feeling of accomplishment as he looked at the bit of gleaming corral they had already put up.

Dexter and Sipe were not having a holiday, either, as Sully had them cutting and raking hay. True to his nature of being fair, Sully had worked them through Sunday also, presumably so they would not have a day off when the woodcutting crew didn't.

Now it was Saturday again, and Sully had said the boys could have Sunday off. Sipe and Dexter did not get in until almost sundown, as they wanted to finish the hay field they were working on. Sipe said he was even too tired to cheat at cards this evening, and the others agreed that they could do without a card game this Saturday night.

Sunday was more or less a day of rest. The bunkhouse hands lazed around after breakfast, then tended to such things as bathing, shaving, and washing clothes. In the afternoon, Quinn spent a little while fidgeting over a letter to Sarah, but he got nowhere on it. After half an hour of staring at the blank sheet of paper, he put it away and turned to the other punchers. Newman sat on the edge of his bunk in stocking feet, oiling his boots. Dexter was sewing a button onto one of his faded blue shirts, and Sipe was sharpening his pocketknife.

"You keep yours good and sharp, don't you?" he said to Newman.

"Oh, yeh," Newman answered. "Keep your guns loaded, and your canteens full."

Sipe tested the edge of the blade with his right thumb. "Is that some of that there wisdom from Comanche country?"

Newman laughed. "Yeh, I suppose so. That, or old trapper talk." Newman's voice changed to an imitation of an old-timer. "Watch yer topknot, child. They's redskins about."

Sipe gave a little laugh. "Those old coons are half Injun themselves. There's still some of 'em up in the high country."

"Probably always will be," said Dexter. "They go from one thing to another—trap out the beaver, shoot the buffalo." He looked at Quinn. "I guess they did a lot of wolfin' up in Montana, didn't they?"

Quinn nodded. "From what I heard. I didn't do any."

Sipe had rolled up his left sleeve. Now he

dropped a gob of spittle on the back of his left wrist and scraped with his knife blade. "They keep at it," he said. "Some of 'em got it in their blood to hunt and trap. Even around here, they trap cats and kah-oats all winter."

"Yeh," said Dexter, "they get to where they can't smell themselves."

An image came to Quinn's mind—a shade of gray and shadow, and a stubbled cheek. "We met one of them the other day," he said. "He didn't smell so bad at the time, did he, Miles?"

Newman looked up from oiling his boots, as if he wasn't used to hearing his first name. "Oh, no." He looked at Sipe and Dexter. "Man name of Blair. Said he ran some stock and did some trappin' in the winter."

Sipe and Dexter both nodded but said nothing.

"No bad smell about him at the time," Newman continued.

Quinn laughed, remembering the whiff of the open flask. "No," he said, "his whiskey smelled plumb fine."

"Neighborly sort," Newman commented.

Dexter and Sipe just nodded.

Newman held up a boot. "I believe leather goes to hell pretty fast in this country. I got these boots wet down there at the river, and look at all these little cracks."

Sipe raised his eyebrows. "That's why us sheepherders always keep a chunk of mutton tallow handy. Good for the cracks in your hands, the cracks in your boots—"

75

Newman laughed. "I should try some."

At that moment, Moose appeared at the door of the washroom that separated the bunkhouse from the cookshack. He took a cigarette from his mouth and said, "Cut out that sheepherder talk, Sipe. Sully's on his way over, and he looks like business."

Sipe looked up. "Really?"

"Uh-huh. I told him I was gonna bake an apple pie, and I think he smelled it."

Newman raised his chin and asked, "Is it cool enough to eat?"

"It sure is," Moose answered. "I've already cut it into six pieces."

On Monday morning, Sully sent the four riders out to check on the range again. As Quinn brushed and saddled the roan horse, he formed an idea of Sully's method of management. It had been nearly two weeks since the last time out, and the owner of the Lockhart Ranch apparently liked to keep current on the state of the range. Quinn could see that Sully was not going to make the mistakes that the absentee owners made in the 1870s and 1880s. A fond idea in the early days, especially in the promotional literature, was that the cattle and the range took care of themselves, and all the investor had to do was brand in the spring to show possession and round up in the fall to harvest the profits. It was a naive idea, and it fell prey to harsh weather, overgrazing, corrupt management, and rustling. The famous bad winter of 1886–87 was now rooted in the mind of the cow country, as were the problems with rustling, which reached their peak a few years later.

The bad weather always loomed as a threat, and people who expected the worst would be the best prepared. Sully was doing what more and more ranchers were doing—putting up hay and planning to manage the herd for winter feeding. For the careful rancher, two roundups a year, several months apart, were not enough for a man to keep track of what he owned and how it was faring.

Quinn had grown into the notions of the country, or had let them grow into him. If it was a good idea to assume that fatal weather was always subject to return, it was also a good idea to assume that rustlers were not just going to go away and get honest jobs baking bread and delivering milk. As long as there were men who thought they could live by their wits, and as long as there was unfenced country for them to work, there would be human predators in the shadows of the distant hills and buttes.

Sully rode the range himself, sporadically and alone, but he relied on the observations reported by his men. Quinn imagined the boss saw enough for himself that he could assess the reliability of each man's impressions. Sully would know a fresh brand when he saw it, and he would not need to smell burnt hair on a man to know if he was an inside operator. In the meanwhile, he seemed to trust his men and he left them to do their work.

That was Sully, Quinn thought—the wide-set eyes that didn't miss much, the rawhide lariat coiled neatly against the saddle. Maybe he was a little dry, as Newman had said, in not caring for liquor or women, but he knew cattle and horses and men, and he didn't need a stool pigeon.

When Quinn had finished saddling the roan horse, he slipped on the bridle and led the horse out into the fresh morning. Newman came out a few minutes later, leading the sorrel with the narrow blaze and two white socks.

Quinn and Newman were riding out together once again on this Monday morning. Quinn understood that if two men worked well together, Sully kept them that way. This morning, Quinn and Newman rode side by side for only a mile or so, then drifted apart to cover more country. Now that Quinn knew the lay of the land, he was on his own like the other riders.

The rangeland had not changed much in two weeks, but Quinn could see that the grass was beginning to dry at the tips. The dust seemed to rise a little higher from the horses' hooves, and as the sun rose, the air itself seemed even drier than before. Off to the west, ahead of him as he moved with the motion of the horse, the dark mountains rose as always, but now in a thicker veil of summer haze.

He imagined it was cooler in the mountains, with shady timber and running water. A splash of water woke a man up on a sleepy afternoon, and chilly air helped him sleep at night.

Quinn thought of Sipe, who had ridden east this

morning. When Sipe doubled back and around, he too would be headed toward the mountains. Quinn smiled as he pictured the pygmy Indians and greasy white men that the mountains seemed to hold for the good-natured cowhand Sipe. Quinn supposed there were lots of range riders down here on the plains who looked up and saw something in the dark lifts of the timbered range.

Quinn's horse stopped, bringing Quinn's thoughts back down to the present time and place, dust and grass and sagebrush. He scanned the ground first, thinking there might be a snake. Then his gaze lifted, and he saw what had stopped the horse. A hundred yards ahead, where the trail sloped down into a gentle draw, stood a mule deer doe and her fawn. Large-eared and black-nosed, they stood broadside with their heads turned toward the horse and rider. They were a drab brown and they looked in good shape, with healthy coats and full bodies. Quinn had not seen any deer since he had come to the Lockhart Ranch, not even when he was at the river, and it made him happy to see these two in good condition. A fawn was always a good sign, anyway. Quinn smiled as he sat and watched.

Then the doe flicked her black tail and sprang into motion, bounding away in the four-legged bounce of the mule deer. The fawn was right behind her, the two of them bouncing away in the distance with their yellow rumps moving up and down in the morning sunlight.

Quinn touched his spurs to the horse, and in a

moment the world was back in motion with the creak of saddle leather, the thud of hooves on dry ground, the passing clumps of sagebrush, and the gradually changing shape of the earth.

In the afternoon, Quinn and Newman saddled fresh horses and rode north as before. Earlier in the day, Quinn had glanced toward the north and had thought of the dark-haired woman he had seen, and he had wondered if he would have to flip a coin to get another chance at seeing her. Now, as he and Newman set out after midday dinner, Quinn headed his bay horse to the left side of the trail. Newman gave no indication of interest in taking that side, and Quinn imagined there might be something over on the east side that Newman would like to take a look at.

In the short while that Quinn had come to know him, Newman seemed to have the normal interests of a cowhand—women, horses, cattle, and liquid refreshment, with the order of importance determined by the circumstances of the moment. There weren't many women in this country, and even fewer single women, so passing up a chance to see one was noteworthy.

Quinn thought it possible that Newman was on the lookout for some profitable human contact, since he seemed to be interested in an opportunity to add to his summer wages. He had sounded out Blair readily enough, and there might be someone to the east who represented a similar interest. For a moment Quinn considered the

80

idea that Newman might know someone who rode the lariat trail in the hills and buttes farther east, but he rejected the notion. For one thing, Newman was working for honest wages and let it be known he needed a stake, so it was unlikely he would do something underhanded and foul his nest. For another, Quinn didn't want to develop the habit of suspecting a fellow cowpuncher. It was better to trust him until he had reason not to.

Quinn rode to the north and hooked around to the west, retracing the route he had followed before. He liked to go the same way the second time he crossed a piece of country, to etch the main features more clearly in his mind and to notice new details he might have missed. He passed the same two wheatfields he had seen earlier. The standing wheat was turning yellow now, and the bare ground lay as before, with a scattering of green weeds sticking up out of the gray dirt.

Before long he came to the place where he had seen the ranch house, and he felt his heartbeat quicken. He had determined that if he saw someone he would ride into the yard and introduce himself, and now he put himself through the idea again, to reinforce his nerve.

Down the slope he rode, taking notice of the house, the stable to the north and set slightly back, the corral to the north of the stable and reaching east. To the left of the stable sat a smaller shed, perhaps a granary or a woodshed, and almost directly in back of the house was the little house that no one liked to have to walk to on a winter night.

He saw no activity in the yard, so he fixed his gaze on the weathered house. In a moment he could see the south side of the house, and he felt a sinking feeling in his middle as he saw no clothes and no woman. Then, glancing back, he saw someone step out of the stable.

He knew that any move on his part would be obviously deliberate anyway, so he just followed his earlier determination and turned the bay horse back toward the house. He saw soon enough that it was a woman's figure, and as she moved out into the open he saw her dark hair. A horse followed her out of the stable. She must have been leading it with her right hand, for she raised her left hand to wave at her oncoming visitor.

Quinn waved back. He could feel his heart thumping and his mouth turning dry. This was it, he thought. He had to meet her now. In a couple of more weeks he might be at the other end of the range, with Sipe and Dexter up north, flipping a coin.

The woman stood waiting with both hands now on the lead rope of the horse. She wore a charcoal-gray shotgun riding skirt and a long-sleeved white blouse. Her long dark hair lay against her shoulders and made a pretty contrast with the white blouse.

The horse was a buckskin, a dun-colored horse with a black mane and tail. It was a medium-size horse, not long-legged and not chunky. It looked fresh and did not have the marks of having been saddled and ridden today.

Quinn's eyes went back to the woman, who stood poised with the lead rope in her hands and the horse behind her right shoulder. As she raised her left hand to brush back her hair, she squinted in a half-smile against the afternoon glare.

"How do you do," he called out, as more of a statement than a question.

"Good afternoon," she answered back.

He rode the last twenty-five yards without speaking, then drew up short of her and said, "I thought I'd drop in and say hello."

"Good," she said, in a voice that didn't really say good or bad.

Quinn swung down from the saddle so that he wouldn't be talking down to her. "Name's Travis Quinn," he said, taking off his hat. "I ride for Sully Lockhart."

As she nodded, her dark eyes seemed to be taking in his features.

"I passed by here a couple of weeks ago and waved, but I didn't take time to stop. The day it rained."

"I'm Marie Delevan," she said, stepping forward and offering her right hand. "I remember you now. I was taking in the wash."

Quinn smiled as he took her firm hand and released it. "We had a pretty good shower right after that."

Her face relaxed a little. "Yes, we did."

A noise at the stable door caused her to look around, and as she did, Quinn took a look at her. She had a medium build, not quite slender. The blouse and skirt fit her loosely, but he could see she had some shape. The twin peaks of her blouse sent a stir through him, and he averted his eyes, first to the horse and then back to her rich, dark hair.

"Come here, honey," she said, backing away from the horse and holding her right hand down and out.

Quinn followed the motion and saw a little boy stepping out of the shadowed doorway. He was a young one, big enough to walk but small enough to still need square pants. He had light brown hair and eyes, and after shooting a glance at Quinn he lowered his gaze and walked quickly to stand behind his mother.

"This is Sam," she said, looking at Quinn and then back at the boy. "Come on, Sam. This is Mr. Quinn."

Quinn put on his hat as he knelt, still holding the reins in his right hand. He spoke to the boy, clearly and deliberately. "Just call me Quinn," he said. "My first name's Travis, but everyone calls me Quinn. You can, too."

The little boy stayed in back of the dark gray skirt.

"Come on," said the woman, bending to him and giving him a nudge, "Say hello to Mr. Quinn." She looked around and said, "As you can see, he's shy."

Quinn stood up. "It's all right. Probably a good way to be."

She nodded but said nothing. Silence hung in the air for a moment until she said, "You can water your horse if you like."

His head went back a little, involuntarily, and as his hat brim went up he winced at the sun. "Thanks," he said. "I didn't want to trouble you at all. I just thought I'd stop by and introduce myself."

"I'm glad you did," she answered. "It's good to know some of the riders who pass by. Especially when they're neighbors." She pointed at the corral. "There's a water trough right inside there."

"Thanks." Quinn led the bay horse through the open gate and let the animal drink. He did not look at the woman again until he led the horse back into the yard. "Obliged," he said, touching his hat. "I suppose I should be on my way."

"Don't be in a hurry," she said. "I'm sure you're thirsty, too."

Quinn shrugged. "I guess so." His mouth was still dry, but not as dry as it had been a little earlier.

"If you hold my horse," she said, "I can be more hospitable."

Quinn took the lead rope and watched her walk away, leading the little boy.

In a few minutes she came out of the house alone, carrying a small tin pail with a dipper sticking out of it. Quinn handed her the lead rope and took the pail.

"Thank you," he said. He dipped himself a drink and then a second one, wiped his mouth on his sleeve, set the dipper back in the pail, and set the pail on the ground. "Thanks," he said again. Then, as he sorted his reins prior to mounting up, he added, "It was nice to meet you."

She looked at him, and the dark eyes did not seem hard or soft. "Yes," she answered, "it was nice to meet you, too."

He led the bay horse away from where she stood with the buckskin. He turned the horse and swung aboard, facing Marie as he settled into the saddle. Touching the brim of his hat, he said, "So long."

"So long, Mr. Quinn."

"Just Quinn, if you don't mind. And please tell Sam I was happy to meet him, too."

She smiled as she brushed hair from her face. "I will." Then she raised her hand in a wave. "So long, Quinn. Don't be afraid to drop in again."

"I will. I mean, I won't be afraid, and I will drop in." He touched his hat again. "Good-bye, Mrs. Delevan."

She smiled again. "Marie," she said, with an evident tone of firmness.

"Good-bye, Marie."

"Good-bye, Quinn. We'll see you later."

He reined the horse around and rode away. He

turned once and looked back. The pail was still sitting on the ground, and she was brushing the buckskin horse. The next time he looked back, the weathered ranch house had closed off both the horse and the woman from his view.

Quinn patted the bay horse on the neck. "A little boy," he said. "I wasn't expecting that."

That evening in the bunkhouse, Quinn let it be known that he had met Marie and the little boy, Sam. He said to Sipe, "You didn't tell me about the little boy."

"Oh, he's just a little spud," Sipe answered. "I didn't even think of him."

Newman, who was shuffling a deck of cards by himself, looked across at Quinn. "Sipe wanted it to be a surprise for you."

Quinn gathered from Newman's tone that he thought of the little boy as a disadvantage to the woman's eligibility. Some men were like that, Quinn thought, and it was understandable. "Well, it *was* a surprise," he said.

Newman cut the deck and showed Quinn the jack of hearts. Then he buried the card, shuffled the deck, cut it, set the bottom half on top, tapped the top card, and turned it over. It was the jack of hearts.

"What became of the little boy's father?" Quinn asked.

The bunkhouse was silent for a moment until Dexter said, "He died of lead poisoning."

Quinn looked at Sipe, who added, "In a saloon

in Douglas." Sipe turned his pipe upside down and rapped it twice on his palm. "Old trouble."

"Oh," said Quinn.

Dexter spoke again. "He was one of the boys they brought in for that trouble up in your old country."

Quinn understood him to mean Johnson County. "Uh-huh."

Sipe had his left palm up, with ashes in it, and his little finger digging into the bowl of the pipe. "And that's the story on Mr. Frank Delevan. He came and he went."

"I see," said Quinn. He turned to Newman, who was inspecting the backs of the cards. "And how was your ride, Miles?"

"Oh, nothing to speak of."

"Sipe saw that herd of wild horses," Dexter said.

Quinn looked at Sipe, who said, "South of here."

Newman looked up from his cards. "Does anyone ever try catchin' 'em?"

"About one out of ten is worth it," Dexter answered. "And there's only five in that bunch."

"They're nothin' but trouble," Sipe added.

Newman wrinkled his nose and went back to shuffling cards.

That night, as he lay in his bunk, Quinn thought some more about Marie. It occurred to him that she might have asked him to call her by her first name because her husband was a hardcase, not because she wanted to be on familiar terms.

He closed his eyes and saw her as he had seen her in the afternoon. Regardless of what her husband might have been like, she wasn't a hard woman. She wasn't helpless and girlish, though, either—not like Sarah. She was a full woman, no doubt about that. And if a fellow ever forgot it, there was a little boy hanging on to her skirt as a reminder.

Chapter Six

Quinn pulled the brace and bit away from the post, leaned forward to blow the shavings out of the hole, then bent at the knees so he could peek through it. It was a good, clean hole—round and straight and ready for a hinge bolt.

He and Newman had been building corrals for two weeks, and Quinn could look around and see the progress. Running the sides up took a little while, especially setting the posts, but the most time went into setting the corners and building the gates. Sully had planned a large corral on the outside, which was where the cattle would come in first from the range or pastures. Then he had two smaller corrals, with a system of gates between all three. Quinn and Newman were now working on the last gate, which would be the first one going in.

They finished hanging the gate in time for noon dinner. Sipe and Dexter were cutting hay quite a ways out, so they had carried a cold meal with them. Sully came into the bunkhouse, hung his hat without comment, and sat down at the table to eat. Quinn and Newman finished cleaning up and sat down at their usual places. No one spoke, and the only sounds were the clacking of silverware on the thick crockery plates. With two men gone, the meal was even quieter than usual.

Quinn heard the door of the bunkhouse open, then boot heels across the floor toward the mess area. He looked up and saw a large man in the doorway. The wide-brimmed hat cast a shadow on the man's face, but Quinn recognized him right away as Blair.

The man's voice came out strong. "Hello, Sully," he said. "Boys."

Quinn and Newman both nodded and said hello.

Sully turned his wide-set eyes on the visitor. "Hello, Blair. Have a seat and dig in." He pointed with his fork at the platters of fried steak and fried potatoes that Moose had placed on the table.

"Thanks," said Blair, moving to a seat next to Sully and across from the other two. He blinked and looked around, then got up and went to the sideboard for a plate and other utensils. He sat down again, still without taking off his hat.

"How are things down your way?" Sully asked.

Blair scraped a heap of potatoes onto his plate. "Just fine. Cattle are fine, grass looks good." He set the platter back onto the middle of the table. "Could use some more rain, though."

"Uh-huh."

Blair spoke across the table as he lifted the platter of steak. "Nice corral you boys are buildin'."

"Thanks," said Quinn.

Blair went to work on his meal, and the room went quiet again.

When Sully was finished eating he put his knife and fork on his plate, stood up and drained his coffee cup, and carried the tableware to the dishpan. As he put on his hat he said, "Was there anything in particular, Blair?"

The guest looked up and around, blinking as the shadow left his face. "Nope. Just a social visit."

Sully looked at his two men and back at Blair. "Good enough. I'll leave you boys to your visit, then." He looked back at Quinn and Newman. "When you get done pickin' up the wood scraps and puttin' everything away, bring in the horse herd and give them all a lookin' over. Some of 'em may need to have their feet trimmed."

"Will do," said Newman.

Quinn nodded.

When Sully was gone, Quinn looked at Blair. The man wore a gray cotton shirt, and as before he had several days' worth of stubble on his cheeks. The jaws bulged as he shoveled in food. When he looked up, he blinked again, and Quinn noticed the washed-out color of the blue-gray eyes.

Blair spoke. "I sure wish I had you boys at my place."

"Why's that?" asked Newman.

Blair laughed. "I been diggin' a root cellar. I could use the help."

"Should be nice an' cool down in there," said Newman, smiling.

"Not so far. I been diggin' it from the top down, and it's hot, dirty work."

Quinn smiled. "When you get it all covered over, though, it should be a nice place to take a snooze."

"I hope so." Blair grinned at both of them. "Temperature should be just right for a jug or two of spirits."

Newman laughed. "Tryin' to hire us away from Sully?"

"Oh, no," Blair answered, looking back down at his plate. "Just makin' pleasant talk."

"I could enjoy droppin' by and watchin' you work," Newman bantered. He got up and carried his plate to the wreck pan, then sat down and poured himself another cup of coffee.

Blair said, "Umm-hmm," around a mouthful of food.

Newman pushed his chair back from the table, put his right ankle up on his left knee, and took out his bag of tobacco. He hefted the makin's in his hand and then said, "Well, what news?"

Blair drank from his coffee. "Ran into an old friend of yours."

Newman paused from opening the neck of the bag, then turned his widened eyes at Blair. "Is that right?"

Blair grinned and looked at Quinn. "Actually, a friend of both of yuh's. Man name of Cater."

The image of a blond man on a gray horse flashed through Quinn's mind. "Did he get on with an outfit hereabouts?"

"Been hangin' around Hartville."

"Good for him," said Newman, now pouring tobacco into the trough he had made of the cigarette paper. He pulled the draw string with his teeth and said, "How did you know he was our friend?"

Blair looked up and squinted. "He mentioned you both. Said he'd been through here and met the two of you."

"Oh," said Newman. "Nothing but kind comments, I'm sure."

Blair laughed. "I didn't put much stock in it. He said you cut his saddle cinch for no reason." Blair looked at Quinn. "And he said you got fired up in the Powder River country, and then you came down here and Newman weaseled you a job."

Quinn felt something flare up inside him. "He can go to hell. I can get a job and keep a job myself." Then he tried to calm himself down as he looked at Newman. "Miles did put in a good word for me, but my work speaks for itself."

"You bet it does," said Newman. "We saddle our own horses and take our own spills. To hell with that pup. We can't worry about what someone like him says."

Blair talked around a mouthful of steak. "I don't think anyone listens to him very much."

Newman licked the cigarette and smoothed it. "Just as well," he said.

When Blair was gone, Quinn and Newman spent the rest of the afternoon as Sully had told them—stacking wood scraps on Moose's woodpile and then looking over the horse herd. That evening, as Dexter sat at the table reading a letter out loud to Sipe, Quinn and Newman went outside to sit by the front door.

"Doesn't it just burn you, though?" said Quinn. "Some fool comes through, ties up his horse like a greenhorn, and then holds someone else at fault when he can't get a job."

"His hot-jawin' 'll just get him in trouble, that's what. I'd say hell with him, and just try to forget him."

For the next few days, Sully put Quinn and Newman to work building a barbed-wire fence around an area where the men would stack hay.

"I never liked this stuff," said Newman, holding his end of the crowbar that ran through the spool of barbed wire. "It goes right through leather gloves."

Quinn, who had also gotten a few gashes in spite of his careful handling, said, "You see more and more of it. But it should keep the cattle off the haystacks." He could see that he and Newman had settled into being Sully's crew for building corrals and fence, while Sipe and Dexter were the haying crew. He also knew that when it came time to bring in the hay, he and Newman would be handling pitchforks.

It just about all came around to steel, he thought. There were the railroads, the fences, and the plows; the guns and knives and traps; the mowing machines and hay rakes; the ax head, the shovel blade, and the pitchfork tines. Riding and roping were different, he thought. Then you were dealing with horseflesh, leather, and hemp. That was the kind of work all of them liked the best, but anyone who wanted to stay working was likely to end up with a piece of steel like this crowbar in his hand.

That evening, all four of the hands sat outside the bunkhouse in the shade and cool of evening. A stray dog had been bumming scraps from Moose for a couple of days, and now it went nosing around the feet and trouser legs of the hired hands.

"I don't like this yella sonofabitch," said Newman, kicking at the dog.

The mongrel snarled back, and Newman lifted the toe of his boot under the dog's jaw, clicking its mouth shut. The yellow dog drew back and sprang forward, still snarling, and put its teeth into the cuff of Newman's right trouser leg.

Newman's chair came down on all fours as he stood up and tried to kick the dog away. "Sonofabitch," he said, and with his right fist he smacked the dog on the side of its head. The dog still hung on, so Newman reached down and settled his hands on the dog's throat. In a few seconds the dog let go, and Newman dragged it out into the dust by the hitching rail. The dog was trying to bite the man's arms, but Newman had a good purchase under the dog's jaws. Quinn could see the man's thumbs pressed into the dog's throat.

Newman lifted the dog and slammed it on the ground. As it pushed back up onto its legs he lifted it and slammed it again. On the third slam it started yelping, and after another slam Newman let it go. Still yelping, the dog began to drag itself away by its front feet as its hind quarters dragged in the dust. It looked as if Newman had broken the animal's back.

Moose's voice came from the door of the cook-shack. "Go ahead and shoot it, Sipe. Get rid of it."

Sipe dashed into the bunkhouse and came out with his six-gun as the dog continued its yowling.

"Would you let me have that?" Newman called out above the noise. "I can finish what I start."

Sipe looked at Newman and handed him the gun.

Newman held the pistol at arm's length, as if he had handled it a hundred times. Quinn saw the cylinder move as the hammer went back under Newman's thumb, and then the blast of the gun-shot marked an end to the noise. The dog lay in a yellow heap on the ground.

Quinn looked across the yard in time to see Sully turn and go back into the house.

Newman handed the revolver back to Sipe. "Thanks," he said.

Sipe nodded and took the gun back into the bunkhouse. Newman followed him in and came out a minute later, pulling on his leather gloves. "I'll get a piece of rope and drag him way the hell off so the magpies can have him," he said.

When Sunday came around, Sully gave the boys a day off. It had been two weeks since their last day off, so their spirits were up as they bathed and shaved.

Dexter and Sipe said they wanted to go up north to drink some cold beer, and they invited

Quinn and Newman to go along. Newman said he would just as soon take a rest, so Quinn said he would stay at the ranch as well.

When Sipe and Dexter were gone, Quinn told Newman he didn't realize he was so tired.

"It's not that I'm that tired," Newman said. "But those boys are goin' to a hog ranch, and I don't want to be throwin' my money away on pissy whiskey."

"Oh."

About half an hour later, Newman yawned and then stood up from his bunk. "I think I might take a ride down and visit our friend Blair. What do you think? Do you want to go along?"

Quinn thought for a second and shook his head. "No, thanks."

Newman grinned. "You thinkin' about goin' to pay Mrs. Delevan a visit?"

Quinn smiled. "Thanks for the suggestion. I would never have thought of it."

Quinn roped out a sorrel horse and saddled it as Newman did the same with a dark horse from his own string. They rode out of the ranch yard together and then split up, Quinn riding north and Newman riding south.

The Delevan ranch lay at about an hour and a half's ride from the Lockhart. Once he was on his way, Quinn realized it would have been a good time to exercise his own horse, but he had followed Newman's lead without thinking. Quinn shrugged and rode on. He did not push the sorrel horse, for it was midmorning now and the day was warming up. All the way along the ride, though, he was anxious to see the woman Marie again. He worried that she might not be home, or worse yet, that she would give him a lukewarm reception.

The first sign of life he saw as he approached the house was the little boy, Sam, who sat playing in a sliver of shade on the north side of the house. In another moment the woman came out of the house and stood in the sunlight. Quinn saw her dark hair shining, and then he saw her right hand go up to shade her eyes.

Closer in, he waved. She waved back and then moved close to the house to stand in the shade.

She was smiling as he rode into the yard. "You made it back," she said.

"Sully keeps his men busy," he said as he swung down.

She moved into the sunlight and said, "So I've heard."

Quinn took a quick glance. The woman was wearing blue cotton trousers and a pale blue, long-sleeved blouse with a flat collar. Her dark hair lay loose against her shoulders as before, and her overall shape was pleasing to the eye.

He moved his eyes to the left, where the little boy was pushing a block of wood as if it were a wagon. "Hello, Sam," he said.

Sam looked up and said nothing.

"Say hello to Mr. Quinn," said the mother.

Sam looked back at the ground.

"He still doesn't know you very well." Marie smiled. "Can I offer you something? Coffee? Water?"

Quinn fidgeted with his reins. "I could stay long enough for a cup of coffee, if it's not too much trouble."

"Not at all," she said. "I'll be back out in a few minutes." She turned and went into the house, leaving Quinn to water and tie up his horse.

She came back outside, closing the door behind her. "The coffee will be a few minutes," she said. She looked around and with a backward motion of her hand toward the stable she said, "There's a little more shade over there."

Quinn nodded and followed her to the stable door, then waited as she went in and brought out two wooden boxes. She set them on either side of the doorway.

"My furniture," she said, with a light laugh.

Quinn gave what he hoped was a smile of approval, then took off his hat and sat down as she did.

After a long moment of silence, she clasped her hands on her right knee and said, "Well, tell me about yourself, Mr. Quinn."

He felt himself wince. "Well, I'm not sure where to begin. Like I told you before, I work for Sully Lockhart. Just been here about a month."

She smiled and nodded, as if she was used to helping boys talk. "And before that?"

Quinn hesitated. "I was up in Montana for a few years. Then I worked in the Powder River country for a little while before I came here."

Marie nodded. "Then I take it you like your work, or you wouldn't still be at it."

100

"Oh, sure," he said. "Some parts of it I like better than others, but it all seems to suit me."

"Did you grow up in Montana?"

"No," he answered without hesitation. "My father was a station agent, and I was born in Julesburg."

"Oh. Down south of here, and east. In Colorado."

"That's right. We moved along the railroad line there, and then when I got older I went out on my own."

"Do you miss it?"

Quinn thought. "We didn't stay in one place long enough to really call it home. I can't say I miss any of it a whole lot. Mostly I remember it as a life that was run by the clock, the telegraph, and the train whistle."

She smiled and nodded, then opened and reclasped her hands. "Are your parents alive?"

Quinn shook his head. "They've both gone on since I left home." Then, to keep her from having to say anything more on that part of the topic, he asked, "And yours?"

"My parents live in Santa Fe," she answered. "They want me to move back, but I've haven't decided to give up on things here yet."

"Oh."

"As you probably know," she went on, "I was married until my husband died."

"I heard that," he said, rotating his hat in his hands. "I was sorry to hear it."

"It's been over a year," she answered, without much of a delay. "I think I have done my grieving. Now I need to decide what is best for my son and me."

Quinn followed her glance to the little boy, who was still playing in the shade. "I imagine it's been hard," he said.

She gave a half-smile and shook her head lightly. "It was not easy when Frank was alive. Then one Saturday night he didn't come back, and things got harder." She raised her head and took a breath. "Now I think I might be through the hardest part."

"I hope so." Quinn looked at her eyes, dark like pools of water in a mountain stream.

Her face relaxed. "I've got my little boy," she said. "That's the greatest joy God could give me, and I haven't lost that. Like my father always told me, you have to take the bitter with the sweet."

Quinn glanced at the boy again and said, "Uh-huh."

Marie rose from her seat. "Excuse me," she said. "I think the coffee might be ready."

Quinn had smelled the wood smoke and had assumed she had stoked the cookstove. "Go ahead," he said.

She came out of the house with two cups of coffee on a pewter tray. After speaking to the boy she crossed the yard to the shade of the stable.

Quinn thanked her and took his cup from the tray. As she sat down, he said, "If you don't mind my asking, what was your name before?"

"My maiden name? It was Vernalle." She looked across at him. "My father comes from a French family, and my mother is Spanish." Then, as if to make the explanation complete, she said, "My father is a saddle-maker."

Quinn didn't have an answer or another question, so he sipped his coffee. After another moment he asked, "Do you have help runnin' your place?"

"I don't have much to run." She motioned with her head toward the range. "I've got a few head of cattle out there, and I paid a couple of other ranchers to do my roundup work along with theirs." She looked at Quinn and then said, quickly, "I know it's not the wisest way to do things, but it got me through the first year."

Quinn nodded.

"Actually," she said, "it didn't get me through as far as money was concerned."

Quinn shrugged, thinking to himself that it was her business and none of his.

"I sold his guns," she said in a steady voice. "Frank had quite a collection of rather valuable rifles and pistols, and I decided to have them sold." Her eyes met Quinn's. "I tell you this because I know you would naturally wonder how a woman gets by with not much of a ranch."

Quinn shrugged again.

"So I sold his guns. I didn't think Sam needed that legacy, anyway."

Quinn glanced at the boy and back at the woman.

She flicked her eyebrows and spoke again. "I sold a few extra horses, too, and a fancy saddle with silver trimmings. I kept a couple of gentle horses for my use, and that's it."

"I didn't mean to be prying—"

"Not at all. None of this is secret. Everybody in the country knows how I've scraped by, and it probably does me some good to say it out loud."

Quinn looked out at the range and then back at her. "Well, I hope things go well for you. If you keep good track of your cattle, you could build up."

She smiled. "I know. I just haven't decided whether I want to try. I could hire a foreman to go out and keep an eye on the gathering and branding, and I think I could make a ranch out of this place if I wanted."

"You'd need someone you could trust," he said, realizing as he said it that he was stating the obvious.

"Oh, yes. And that would take a little doing."

Quinn thought of Cullen and then Cater. "Country's full of good men lookin' for a job like that," he quipped.

Marie broke into laughter that seemed to be natural to her. "It sure is, isn't it?"

Quinn laughed with her. It wasn't a bad joke, he thought, and it seemed to be doing them both some good. He knew it made him feel good to hear her laugh.

On the way back to the ranch, Quinn had two main impressions that he played back and forth by turns. He recalled how Marie had deflected his expression of sympathy and had spoken matter-of-factly about disposing of her husband's effects. Quinn did not think she was cold about it, but she seemed deliberate in managing her feelings. She was probably done with her grieving, as she had said, and he thought she had a clear way of thinking about it all.

His other impression was of the little boy, Sam. He would be his father's son, and a man who had an interest in the mother would have to take that into account. The boy was still little and could grow under a new influence, but the shadow of his father would always be present, if only in the background. For some men, that was enough reason not to take a second look at the woman. For Quinn, it was a realistic detail. As life presented its possibilities, it reminded a person that the outcome wouldn't be perfect. He smiled. Marie had come to that realization, too.

Chapter Seven

Quinn smelled whiskey in the bunkhouse after Newman came in at about midnight. Sipe and Dexter had come in a little earlier, but their bunks were farther away and the fumes did not carry. When the men got up in the morning and went to the breakfast table, the smell of bacon and coffee was strong enough to block out the odor of alcohol, but when Quinn and Newman were saddling their horses, Quinn whiffed the smell of liquor again. Newman was walking steadily and not slurring his words, but he had the booze on his breath.

Quinn did not mind the smell of liquor, unless someone was rotten drunk, but he did notice it if he hadn't been drinking himself. In this instance he found it almost amusing. Newman might resist throwing his money away on hog ranch whiskey, but he hadn't been opposed to accepting Blair's hospitality.

As they walked their horses out a few steps and then paused to tighten their cinches, Newman said, "How 'bout we switch off today, and you can see some new country. As for the afternoon, you got to see your little Mohee yesterday, and I don't plan to stop by there anyway."

"Fine with me," said Quinn, tucking in the loose end of his latigo. He put the toe of his boot into the stirrup and swung aboard the bay horse.

He looked over at Newman, who swung into the saddle just as easily. The two of them trotted their horses out of the yard, and before long they were a mile apart, riding westward. Quinn wondered if Newman had any motives for switching off today; he wondered if Newman's visit with Blair had anything to do with it.

Quinn had expected they would ride the range again, as it had been a couple of weeks since their last ride. He had already thought it was in his best interests to know more about the country, so he found Newman's suggestion agreeable.

His ride to the west did not turn up any surprises. The cattle were scattered out normally, the grass was a little drier, and the sagebrush seemed more pungent. The dark mountains rose in the west as always—dark and distant and intriguing.

Quinn rested at the farthest point of his ride, as usual. The bay horse was the calmest in his string, so he felt comfortable sitting in its shade without worrying if it was going to jerk the reins out of his hand.

The world around him lay dead silent now—no wind, no birds, no cattle, no people. He was miles from any railroad, which suited him fine. The country stretched out, warming again beneath the midmorning sun. Quinn imagined Newman, a mile or more to the north, also blending in with the surrounding country—and Sipe and Dexter behind him, to the east and south, also small figures beneath the spreading sky. Each was on his own lone journey, his half of a cloverleaf, covering ground where Indians had hunted, buffalo had died, and coyotes had feasted.

The riders passed over it, but the land stayed the same—at least, he thought, until the railroads came, and the plows and the fences. The railroads made the biggest cuts, or the longest. For as much as people blessed and cursed them, the railroads did not change the mantle of the earth as much as a mile or two of fence did. When nesters fenced in streams or waterholes, the cattle trampled the damp ground. Animals grazed a fenced pasture closer than they would an open range, as a person could see by looking at both sides of a fence. And when settlers fenced in land for farming, they broke up the whole face of the earth that once had been continuous or whole.

Quinn had heard that the buffalo were reluctant to cross railroad tracks, just as the early trail herds had been. But a fence stopped everything on foot or wheels. Quinn understood that a man could still ride all the way from Canada to Mexico and not have to get down to open a gate—if he knew where to ride. That would change, and everyone knew it.

For the time being, though, time seemed to stand still and the man-made world seemed far away. Quinn had not seen a fence all morning, nor a person, either, since he had split up with Newman. He had a broad sense of being bordered on the north by a low range of hills, on the east by hills and buttes, on the south and southwest by the river, and on the west by mountains. At times like this, when he was alone on the range, he could forget about the bands and blades of steel as he became part of his surroundings. He could smell the good smell of his horse, feel his own heart beating, and know that he was just blood and bone, paused on one spot of a vast grassland where other creatures had hunted, mated, and died.

Quinn sat pensive for quite a while until he came back to the here and now of his day's work. He rose to his feet, conscious of his leather boots and felt hat, the shining bit in the bay horse's mouth, the warm saddle leather. He checked his cinch, flipped his reins into place, and stepped into the stirrup.

He moved to the south and southwest now, moving toward the broken country he and Newman had gone around on their trips to the river. On previous rides it had been Newman's range, and now Quinn was getting a look at it. He rode along a cattle trail, which generally followed the contours of the land.

At one point the trail led to the right around the base of a bluff. Like other bluffs in this country, it was a face of grayish-tan clay, hard earth that some people called sandstone although it wasn't. Quinn looked ahead at the trail where it curved around the bluff and dropped out of sight. Beyond the bluff, the land fell away into what looked like a shallow valley and then rose to another slope with similar clay outcroppings.

Something inside told him to pause, as it had done the day he met Newman. He could not have said if it was a fleeting image or if it was something more ethereal, but he trusted his inner sense at times like these. He knew it was a good idea, at any rate, to break out of a lull.

He reined the horse to the left of the trail and headed it up the steep, grassy slope that formed the back side of the bluff. Before he got to the ridge he slipped out of the saddle and, holding the reins by the very ends so that the horse would be farther downhill, stepped slowly toward the crest. He took off his hat, put it in his right hand with the reins, and shaded his eyes with his left hand. As his line of vision cleared the rim, he saw the bowl or valley spread out in front of him. He saw nothing but the range itself. The ridge he was standing behind took a sharp rise to his right, obstructing his view on that side, so he stepped forward half a step.

Then he saw a rider, moving below him from right to left on a gray horse. The man wore a light-colored shirt and a dark vest, topped with a dark, round-brimmed hat with a peaked crown. The style of hat was common, but Quinn thought he recognized it. When the rider looked up and around, Quinn saw the yellow hair and mustache and knew it was Cater.

When the rider's hat brim closed off his face again as he looked at the trail ahead of him, Quinn dropped back from the ridge. Whatever Cater was up to, he was out in the open and didn't seem to be skulking along. He seemed to be headed in the general direction of Hartville, and if so, his trail would take him off of Quinn's range before long.

Still walking softly to try to keep his spurs from jingling, Quinn led the bay horse back down the slope. He stepped aboard from an uphill position, then turned the horse east and walked him out slowly. His idea was to ride parallel to Cater with the ridge between them, and thus shave only a corner off the cloverleaf he would have ridden.

After a little while, Quinn gave the horse more rein and let him step out at a faster walk. Cater was probably well ahead of him now and headed south. He did not fear Cater, but he thought it would be just as well if he did not meet up with the man.

Riding on, Quinn continued to wonder what Cater might have been up to. He told himself it was none of his business, that a man had a right to travel across open range. Then it occurred to him that there might be some connection to Newman's change in pattern. Quinn wondered if Blair knew something about Cater and had dropped a hint to Newman. It could be something as innocent as Cater riding for another outfit, or it could be something murkier that Newman would prefer to avoid. Or it could be nothing at all.

Quinn said nothing about it to Newman at midday dinner, but that evening he found an opportunity. Dexter and Sipe stayed at the table after supper, as Dexter was writing a letter for Sipe, and it seemed to be of a delicate nature relating to a young woman in Ohio who had answered an earlier letter from Sipe. In due respect to Cupid, Quinn and Newman took chairs outside and sat in the dusk.

After Newman had rolled and lit a cigarette, Quinn asked, "Have you heard anything new about Cater?"

Newman shook his head. "No. Why?"

"Well, I saw him this morning, out on the south part of my ride."

"I wouldn't doubt it. He doesn't even have a range to be off of. Did he see you?"

"No." Quinn hesitated, then asked, "Do you think he was expecting to run into you?"

Newman shook his head again. "Nah." After a slow drag on his cigarette he said, "Come to think of it, Blair did say somethin', but I didn't give it a second thought, and it was pretty late then."

Quinn nodded, assuming that "late" with Blair meant the haze and blur of whiskey. "Uh-huh," he said, giving Newman the go-ahead.

"Well, he said he'd seen young Galahad out that way, thinkin' he'd put a rope on one of them wild horses. I don't know what he'd do with one if he managed to get it on the end of his rope. He can't even saddle his own horse—but, of course, that don't matter to the likes of him."

Quinn gave it a quick thought. "That sounds

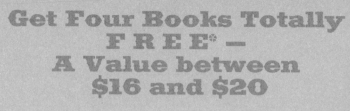

Get Four Books Totally F R E E* – A Value between $16 and $20

Tear here and mail your FREE* book card today!

PLEASE RUSH
MY FOUR FREE*
BOOKS TO ME
RIGHT AWAY!

LeisureWestern Book Club
P.O. Box 6613
Edison, NJ 08818-6613

AFFIX
STAMP
HERE

about right, if he was out on that kind of maneuver. It sounds like he hasn't landed a job yet."

Newman turned down the corners of his mouth. "Kinda hard to do that just layin' around the saloon in Hartville."

Quinn and Newman went back to building fence for the next few days, and then they started moving hay from the fields to the fenced-in areas. They were well into August now, and the heat lay heavy on the country. Sully seemed to have some concern for getting the hay in; he took to riding the range himself and kept all four men at the haying. He also kept them working seven days a week for a solid month. Apparently he was satisfied with the progress by the first Sunday in September, for he gave the men a day off.

All this time, Quinn had thought about writing a letter to Sarah, but whenever he came to the blank sheet of paper he felt he was at a deadlock. Now that he had a day off, he knew he would rather shave and go see Marie than torture himself with a letter he had been unable to write. So he trimmed his beard for length, shaved the edges, and took a soak in the tub. Then he put on a fresh shirt and rode north.

He rode his own saddle horse this time. It was a brown horse, almost matching the dark brown packhorse. Both of his horses had seen little work for the past couple of months, and now that Quinn had the chance, he decided to give one of them some exercise.

Quinn took it slowly so as not to overheat the

horse, and he got to the Delevan place at that time of day when a horse stands on its own shadow. He called out as he rode into the yard, and Marie stepped out of the kitchen door, closing it softly behind her.

"Sam's asleep," she said.

Quinn nodded and dismounted. She was closer now, so he said in a low voice, "How have you been?" He saw she was wearing a light cotton dress, pale yellow, that was snug at the waist. It showed her bosom and her hips to advantage, and he wondered if she was expecting company.

"All right," she answered. "How about yourself?"

"Fine." He took off his hat and said, "I hope this isn't an inconvenient time for me to drop by."

"Not at all."

"Good. I haven't had a day off since I saw you last, and I thought I'd ride over the first chance I got."

Marie's dark eyes sparkled as she smiled. "I heard Sully was putting up a lot of hay. I figured he let you in on it."

He held his left hand palm out and rubbed his thumb across the calluses he had gotten from the pitchfork. "He sure did."

She smiled as she watched him. Then she put her hand up to shade her brow. "It's hot. Shall we sit in the shade?" She looked at the horse. "Go ahead and put him up, and I'll get you something. Coffee or water?"

"Water," he said.

They sat in the doorway of the stable, again on wooden boxes. They went through small talk about the weather, the work behind, and the work ahead.

"You know," she said, "it never seemed as if Frank did all that much, but once he was gone, I got to notice how much he actually did."

"Uh-huh."

She moved her head slowly, side to side. "Sometimes it's hard to believe, even now. It's been over a year, and sometimes I still expect to hear him come riding into the yard." She paused and then continued. "Someone who was that alive, who had that much force in him—" She hesitated.

Quinn didn't know what to say, but words came. "And him bein' the father of your little boy, and all."

"Oh, that too, of course. Probably that more than anything." Her chest rose and fell as she took a breath and exhaled. "My mother told me I would always be married to him, in a way. Through Sam."

Quinn thought he would test the impression he had gathered on his last visit. "That's a big package. Husband and father. You lose a lot." She didn't say anything, so he went on to say, "I've never lost someone like that, but I imagine you must miss him pretty powerfully sometimes."

"I can't say that it's powerful, but there's an ache that comes back. Part of it is just the idea that someone like that will never get to see any of this again." She moved her hand outward toward the rangeland, and then, looking back at Quinn, she furrowed her brow.

Quinn nodded. He realized she had not said

anything endearing about the man himself. He recalled her comment about being done with the grieving, and he thought there must have been something to grieve. "But you still must miss him," he said.

She shrugged. "When I get sad, it's because of my sense of death—that, and because my son doesn't have a father. It's not because I miss him myself." She paused for a second, bit her lower lip, and released it. "You've probably heard some things about Frank."

"Just the bare bones. I heard he'd been in some of that trouble a while back."

"Well, I heard that, too." She paused, and when she spoke again her tone sounded bitter. "But not until after I married him."

"Oh."

She opened her mouth, closed it, and then opened it again to speak. "I hope I didn't make you uncomfortable."

He shrugged. "No, not at all. And like you said last time, it probably does some good to talk about it out loud."

"I suppose I still have some hard feelings. I can hear it in myself. But anyway, this was our little honeymoon cottage," she said, pointing at the house where the little boy was sleeping. "This place was given to him, I found out—as a sort of reward for the work he had done."

Quinn felt a bad taste come to his mouth, and he could feel the expression of dislike spreading through his facial features.

"The next thing to blood money," she said. "But

by then I was married, and then I had a little baby. That's when I understood what my father had always said about taking the bitter with the sweet."

Quinn thought he could dare to say what he thought. "Then you weren't absolutely in love with him as time went on."

She smiled faintly. "As they say, you get to know a person much better when you're married to him. That's when you find out if there's really any trust."

Quinn recalled the earlier conversation, when she said she had sold her husband's guns. Now he could see more clearly why she had had a lingering bad feeling about the man's past. "Uh-huh," he said. "You find out things you should have known sooner."

She waited a few seconds before answering. "It wasn't just that. For him, it was a way of life, not having any trust."

"And not being trusted."

"It comes to that, sooner or later."

They sat in silence for a few minutes until Quinn worked himself up to ask a question. "Do you think you'll go back?" He looked at her dark hair, her smooth, clear face, and the pale yellow shoulders of her dress, pretty as a rose. He knew he hoped she would say no.

"To Santa Fe?"

"Uh-huh."

"I don't know. You'd think I would have sold this place the first chance I got. But it's the one thing I have—for myself and for my son."

Quinn nodded.

"I didn't come from property. I never had it. Now I think sometimes that I should hang on to it and try to make it into something. For me, and for Sam."

"In spite of how it came your way," he suggested.

"It's strange," she said, "but that seems almost to have taken care of itself. While Frank was alive I resented his bringing me to this place that he had gotten the way he did. Like I said, it seemed to be bought with blood. Then, when he died, it seemed to be redeemed the same way." She waved her left hand again at the plains that spread away from the yard. "The land itself doesn't have any guilt," she said. "People do. But they don't really own the country or transfer anything to it. They live on it, and they pass it on. The land goes on being itself. For me, Frank has gone right out of this place. He didn't build this house, or this barn and corral." She met Quinn with her dark eyes.

Quinn let out a breath. "So you could keep the place and try to make a go of it."

She nodded. "Take it on its own. This is an honest place. I've come to have a feeling for it."

Quinn looked out across the country. "I can understand that," he said.

Her voice sounded clear and steady as she said, "It was a big disappointment to learn what I did. But a person can get over it and move ahead."

His eyes met hers, and he answered, "I believe that."

On his way back to the Lockhart Ranch, Quinn heard the sound of a dove. It sounded like a sad call, the long lonely hoots that floated across the dry prairie. The sound seemed to match the feeling he carried with him from Marie's place. Although their conversation had turned to lighter, happier topics, his central feeling was twined up with the ideas of blood, guilt, and redemption. But then, as he heard the dove again, he realized that the bird itself was not necessarily sad. It was called a mourning dove because that was what people heard in the call, just as they heard happiness in the song of the meadowlark.

The bunkhouse was empty when Quinn arrived. Moose had gone with Dexter and Sipe to drink cold beer, as they said, and Newman had gone to see if Blair had finished his root cellar. It occurred to him that he could write a letter if he wanted.

Among the many details Quinn had turned over in his mind on the ride home, one seemed to speak directly to him. It was the comment in which Marie had said that when you marry a person, you find out if there's really any trust. In addition to understanding how Marie could put her life with Frank behind her, Quinn could see how the comment applied to Sarah.

Although there was nothing to distrust about Sarah, he knew he did not have to marry her in order to find out if he should have. He knew deep down that they did not have the basis for a marriage; they didn't really know each other. She had wanted someone to tend to her, and he had wanted to be the person. But she didn't know him, not really, and he didn't know her. When he thought of her he always pictured her indoors, with her clean blond hair and her shiny blue eyes, in a room with porcelain knobs on the sideboard, a brass lamp on the table, pink flowers painted on a water pitcher. In her own life she was undoubtedly more real than the porcelain knobs and painted flowers, but he did not know that part of her. And now he could admit to himself that he didn't care to know her any better.

A cloud seemed to have lifted. He knew what kind of a letter he should write. In it he could say he knew his own heart and mind better now. He could take the blame for saying things too soon. He could apologize for going back on his word, for deciding he would not go to see her in Cheyenne after all.

He knew now that he could write the letter. There was no one around to distract him. He took out the paper and found a pencil to write the first draft. The words did not come easily, but the deadlock was over.

Chapter Eight

Quinn heard the coyotes wailing in the middle of the night, before the chuck wagon cook was up and about. After a few nights on roundup, a fellow got used to the regular sounds of cattle, night herders, bells in the horse herd, and thumps and clangs at the chuck wagon. Usually the cook was at his work by three in the morning, building the fire and mixing dough while the rest of the men tried to steal more sleep.

The first time Quinn heard the coyotes, the camp was still dark and quiet. He snuggled in his bedroll and went back to sleep. When the chorus of wails and yaps woke him the second time, the campfire was built up and a lit lantern hung from a pole on the chuck wagon. A horse stood tied to the left rear wheel of the wagon, and a cowpuncher Quinn didn't recognize right away stood drinking a cup of coffee by the fire. Quinn thought he might be able to catch a few more winks before everyone rolled out, so he turned over and closed his eyes.

Fall roundup had begun in the third week of September. Already the days seemed shorter and the nights cooler, and anyone could feel that frost was not far away. Some of the punchers had sleeping tents, but many of them, including Quinn and Newman, slept on the ground in a bedroll wrapped in a canvas tarpaulin. Newman's bed was not far away; Quinn had not heard him stir either time the coyotes sent up their ruckus.

For most cattlemen, fall roundup meant beef roundup. It was the time to gather the beef for shipping. It was also the time to brand any calves that had been missed in spring roundup or born since then. Those calves, if not branded now or by someone else in the winter, would not be identifiable in the spring because they would no longer be with their mothers. Then they would be full-fledged mavericks. A maverick was a stray calf that hadn't been branded, a calf whose ownership couldn't be determined unless someone put a brand on it.

In addition to gathering beef and branding leftovers, ranchers who planned to feed through the winter used this occasion to push their own stock closer to the ranch. That was Sully's method. He gathered his whole herd and would cut out the beef for shipping a little later on.

Sully had thrown in with two other outfits—the Self and the Singletree—to form a roundup crew.

The Self ranch had provided the chuck wagon and the cook. Sully provided the bed wagon and the day wrangler, Moose. The boss of the Singletree had to hire a couple of extra riders to fill out his part of the crew, and much to Quinn's relief, neither of them turned out to be Cater.

The crew started west of the Lockhart Ranch and moved clockwise to cover the roundup area. Reps, or representatives, from nearby ranches came and went as the roundup moved. They took cattle out of the main herd, but still the herd grew and grew.

So far, the weather had not given any trouble. The men had not had to contend with slippery ground, wet ropes, or frozen ropes. They had had a spell of cool, damp weather just before roundup, and they could expect first frost any day, but for the time being the weather was ideal.

Newman and Dexter turned out to be two of the best ropers on the crew, and they roped most of the calves for branding. Like the majority of the plains cowboys they roped hard and fast, with the rope tied to the saddle horn. Quinn, who had worked mountain ranches, had learned to take his dallies, and he saw other punchers who roped that way. Sipe roped hard and fast, but as he said, not very often. He was a good calf wrestler, adept at flanking these bigger calves. He and Quinn often worked as a pair, holding the calf down while another man came with the hot iron.

Sully always branded his own stock. He knew how hot he liked the iron and how deep to brand according to the age of the animal. Usually he picked his own iron from the fire, but if someone brought him one, he made sure all the hair was burned off from the previous use. His brand consisted of a heart sitting inside an *L,* and his cattle carried brands that anyone could read clearly.

The roundup crew usually started the day with a gather, in which all hands except the day herders rode out to make a big circle drive. At the end of the day they branded, then went to camp, and all the punchers except the reps took shifts at night herding. Quinn assumed that the puncher at the fire was getting ready to relieve the herders who had gone on shift at two in the morning.

Quinn had barely closed his eyes, it seemed, when he heard the cook's call. Quinn rolled out of his bedding and went about his morning routine. After tossing his bedroll into the bed wagon, he made his way to the campfire.

"Let's git to gittin'," said the cook, which he said every morning. "Time's a-flyin'."

As Quinn downed his breakfast, Newman came to the fire. He had ridden relief from twelve to two, so he had probably been in his deep sleep when the coyotes were howling. "Ready to ride?" he said to Quinn, with his usual cheerfulness.

"Yep," Quinn answered. He rose to his feet, shook out his coffee cup, and tossed it along with his fork and tin plate into the wreck pan. There was no ceremony at mealtime, especially in the morning or at midday, when a man ate and went to work.

That evening, after a full day's gather and branding, the Lockhart hands ended up at the campfire, along with half a dozen of the others. What little leisure there was on roundup came at this time.

A puncher from the Singletree, who sat with his arms hugging his knees, looked away from the fire and opened the conversation. "Did you hear them ky-otees last night?"

"Oh, did I," said Sipe. "They're singin' about the end of summer."

"Cold weather's comin'," said another voice. "It's gonna be an early winter."

Quinn looked at the puncher who had just spoken. He was a young man from the Self outfit, probably twenty or so. He had the brim of his hat turned up in front, and the firelight gleamed on his smiling face. Every year at this time, Quinn thought, people started predicting the winter—usually they said it would come early. The young cowhands learned to repeat this sort of wisdom, to make themselves seem more seasoned. The others could speak from experience.

"It'll get cold soon enough," Dexter commented. He had his hat pushed back on his head. It was a worn hat, with a hole forming at the front of the crown where the dents met.

"Come a good snow," said Sipe, "and you'll see them kah-oats out huntin' in pairs."

Dexter turned to Quinn. "They say coyotes will come along after wolves, where the wolves have run animals into the deep snow, and they'll pick up on the leftovers."

Quinn shrugged. "I suppose."

Sipe's voice came back. "Yer kah-oat, he's handy. He'll hunt with another one of his own kind, or he'll hunt with a badger, or he'll go to where the ravens are squawkin'."

"He looks for opportunity," Dexter said. "I've heard that. He'll sit there and watch the badger diggin', and he'll jump what runs out. He's not particular about what he eats."

"Meat's meat," said the young rider with the upturned brim, who had begun to roll a cigarette.

"I believe it about the wolves," Sipe continued, "though I haven't seen it myself. But that's when he listens for the ravens, is in deep snow. So it stands to reason he'd follow the wolves then, too." He rapped his pipe on his boot heel.

The young man looked up from building his cigarette. "I bet we have deep snow before round-up's through."

Dexter turned to Sipe as if to ignore the young puncher. "I think it works both ways with the ravens. They'll come along and take his leavin's, too." Then he looked at the young man. "I doubt we'll have deep snow that soon. This roundup lasts about a month, that's all. But it'll get cold soon enough."

"That's right," Newman chipped in. "Because when it gets cold, that'll be soon enough for me."

The next morning, Quinn had frost on his tarp. It was the twentieth of September, and now there was a familiar quick feeling in the air.

"Let's git to gittin'," called out the chuck wagon cook. "You know those horses are gonna be buckin' every day from now on."

* * *

On the third week of roundup, when the wagons were on the southern swing of the campaign, Blair came to the camp to rep for his own brand. The man had a string of eight horses, including the one he rode and the one that carried his bedroll and warbag. His gray wool coat was tied to the back of his saddle as before. When Blair dismounted and came to the fire, Quinn noticed again the broad-brimmed gray hat, the recessed chin and stubbled cheeks, the slanting forehead, and the squinting eyes. Blair said hello all the way around and made himself at home in camp, serving himself a cup of coffee and then going for a plate of grub.

Before long, Quinn gathered that Newman's two visits to Blair's place had promoted an easy friendship between the two. As Blair was given to laughing heartily and slapping others on the shoulder, his hand often landed on Newman.

After the next day's gather, Quinn thought that Blair might have shared a private nip with Newman before they came back to camp, for they had a delinquent air about them. No one was supposed to drink on roundup, but it was easy to imagine Blair with a flask of contraband.

As the roundup hands finished supper and settled by the campfire, Blair remained his garrulous self, talking and laughing loudly. He made a couple of references to a hunting trip he and Newman were planning to take when the roundup was done.

"Greenhorns and greenbacks," he said. "Isn't that right, cousin?"

"Coin of the realm," said Newman, "if we don't freeze our asses."

Blair wrinkled his nose as he squinted. "It's part of their adventure. It's what they pay for."

The talk went on, and before long it turned to firearms. "Wonderful tool," Blair proclaimed. "It makes its bark here and its bite over there."

"And the bite's a hell of a lot worse," said a puncher from the Singletree.

"It gets there first, too," Newman added.

The young puncher with the upturned brim perked up. "What do you mean?"

Newman pursed his lips and then said, "Well, if a shot comes your way, the bullet gets there before the sound does. I know that much."

Sipe joined in. "That's a fact. And if you're standin' off at a distance an' you see another man shoot an animal, you see the animal fall before you hear the shot."

Blair laughed. "I'd rather be the one pullin' the trigger and be the first to hear the sound, rather than either of them other two."

Newman tossed the pinched end of his cigarette into the fire. "When you hunt with these green-horns, though, I suppose you need to stand back and watch them take their shots, don't you?"

"Sometimes." Blair looked around and gave a broad wink. "But sometimes it's like other things, and you gotta do it for 'em."

Quinn thought there was supposed to be some petticoat humor in the comment, but no one laughed. For as much as Blair seemed at ease around everyone else, sometimes his comments fell on dead air.

After a long moment of silence, Newman spoke up. "I believe we haven't sung 'The Little Mohee' yet this evenin'."

"Not yet," said Blair. "But it sounds like we're goin' to."

Quinn recalled Newman's mention of a little Mohee after a night at Blair's, so he assumed it was a song the new friends had sung together when the juice was flowing. It was a well-known song, originally a sailor song, and most punchers had heard it if not sung it.

Newman sang the first verse by himself, introducing the "young Indian lass." By the second verse, Blair and a couple of others had joined in.

"She came and sat by me and took up my hand;
She said, 'You're a stranger and not from this land.
If you'll settle down and stay here with me,
I'll teach you the language of the little Mohee.' "

Newman laid his hand flat on his chest and sang in a voice louder than the others:

"Oh, no, my dear maiden, this never can be,
For I have a true love in my own country;
And I'll not forsake her for I know she loves me,
And her heart is as true as the little Mohee's."

Then he lowered his voice to the level of Blair and the others, and together they all finished the song:

"Now that I'm back on my own native shore,
With friends and relations around me once more,
With all that's around me, there's none that I see
That's fit to compare with the little Mohee.

"The girl I had trusted proved untrue to me,
So I'll turn my thoughts backward far over the
*   sea;*
I'll turn my thoughts backward and backward I'll
*   flee,*
To spend all my days with the little Mohee."

When the song was over, Sipe made a comment. "I'll tell you, I've heard versions of that song where she lives off on some island in a coconut grove, and then I've heard other fellas say that 'Mohee' is short for 'Mohican.' Really, she could be any little Indian."

"Isn't that the truth," said Newman. "She's a good girl."

The young puncher spoke again. "I bet it don't get cold in a coconut grove."

Newman smiled in the firelight. "Especially if you've got your little Mohee," he said, and everybody laughed.

The next morning, a light skiff of snow lay on the ground. It was the third of October. No one needed to be told now that the horses would be hunching their backs.

Roundup went on, with the wagons moving on to the west and back north. Blair left with his string of horses and a few head of cattle, headed back to his wife and root cellar, Quinn imagined. The bedroll tarps had frost on them almost every morning now, and the coats and gloves came out of the bed wagon.

Newman wore the tan, blanket-lined coat almost all the time. Quinn thought he should try to stand the cold a little more and let his blood thicken, but when he mentioned it, Newman said, "That's what I'm doin'."

Roundup came to an end in the third week of October. Cold wind was whipping out of the northwest when the Lockhart crew brought the herd back to the ranch. It took two days to cut the herd into those cattle going back to the range and those to be shipped for beef. The men turned the shipping steers into a pasture that Quinn and Newman had fenced in after the haying was done. Sully seemed pleased to have the pasture ready, and Quinn, despite his aversion to fences, was glad to see his work coming to a purpose.

Quinn learned that Dexter and Sipe would be kept on the payroll to pitch hay and check cows through the winter. In a couple of days they would take the market steers, throw in with the other two outfits, and drive the beef north to the railroad. Then they would come back for their winter work.

Sully told Quinn and Newman he would pay them through the end of the month anyway, but they were done if they wanted to be. Then he said they were free to stay on at the bunkhouse as long as they wanted. Quinn, who understood the invitation to mean grub but no further pay, said he would stay around for a few days at least, to rest up.

Newman said he would like to move on down to Blair's so the two of them could go out scouting. Their hunting guests would arrive in a couple of weeks, he said, and Blair wanted to go up to the mountains, scout around, and set the camp. Sully paid Newman for the full month and let him go ahead.

After Newman was gone, Sully came back to the bunkhouse and told Quinn not to be in a hurry to leave. He had another little job for him, he said, but he could rest up first.

Quinn agreed and then settled into the tasks that came at the end of roundup—washing and mending clothes, trimming his beard, cutting his toenails, and taking long baths.

Sipe and Dexter had let their beards grow during roundup, but when they came to mess table that evening their faces were smooth and shining. Moose had shaved also, but he had left his mustache.

"I hope you fellas don't get cold on this drive you're goin' on," Quinn teased, stroking his own bearded chin. "I'll be worryin' about you."

"Don't worry about us," Dexter said as he speared a steak. "Once we load the steers, we're gonna go all the way into Chadron and buy winter clothes. Fur caps, and mittens, and the whole show."

"Worry about us later on," said Sipe, "when this whole place turns into a big icebox. You'll be off

132

in a parlor somewhere, with your foot on the radiator, and you can give a thought to your old pals up here, with icicles on our noses."

Quinn laughed.

Dexter spoke again. "I'd worry about Newman. He's not used to this cold, and Blair's gonna take him off and get him froze to death."

Sipe gave a sniff as he cut into his slab of beef. "He said he's gonna buy a fur coat—or Blair's gonna stake him to one, that was it."

Dexter spoke again. "It's too bad Newman didn't have as much of a stake as he needed. I don't know how much good can come out of bein' in cahoots with Blair."

Sipe paused with a chunk of steak on the end of his fork. "Oh, Blair's all right. And Newman can look out for himself."

"I suppose," Dexter said. He looked back at Quinn. "But if there's anyone to worry about, it's him."

"Maybe," Quinn answered. "But I agree with Sipe. I think Newman can take care of himself."

As he said it, he knew what he really thought. In his view, Newman was out to make a profit trading on Blair's know-how, whereas Blair was out to take advantage of his uninitiated helper. It seemed like one of those cases in which each party thought he was a little sharper than the other but was happy not to make an issue of it if there was a third party to fleece. As for whether one of the two, Newman or Blair, might come out ahead, Quinn thought it was even money.

Later, when he was by himself and thought

about it some more, he began to feel that Dexter made sense when he questioned how much good could come out of being in cahoots with Blair. It also raised the question of how honorable Newman might be, especially in the company of the man who called him cousin.

It took Quinn only a day to get caught up on his personal tasks, and after two good nights' sleep he felt well rested. He knew Sully expected him to take at least another day off, so he did, thinking it would be a good time to go see Marie.

He decided to ride his packhorse on this visit. From time to time he had found the time to ride his saddle horse, but the other one had seen little exercise for over two months. He was a docile horse, not the type that would buck and pitch if it hadn't been ridden in a while. Quinn caught the brown horse and saddled it without any trouble, and he was on his way.

He did not push the horse, but it had a good walking pace and the day was cool, so he arrived at the Delevan place by midmorning. The wood shingles on the roof were shining in the autumn sunlight, which seemed at once to be fragile and rich.

Autumn always gave him a feeling of excitement. As the flies died off and the horses got frisky, Quinn felt his blood getting ready for winter. The tension in the air was a good one; it brought vigor to the body after months of hot weather and long working days.

Riding into the yard, he saw no sign of activity. There were no horses in the corral, but that was not unusual. He had noticed Marie often kept her horses in the stable or in the smaller pens behind it.

Just as he was about to call out, he heard a noise in back of the house. It was a thunking noise, the sound of metal on wood. He dismounted and walked his horse to the back corner of the house.

There stood Marie with an ax in her hands, looking at a dry, twisted cedar trunk at her feet. She was wearing a light blue denim work shirt and a pair of gray woolen trousers, and her hair was tied in back of her head with a bandanna.

Quinn made a clucking sound, and she looked up. She shook her head and made a small laugh.

"Rough work?" he asked.

She blew her breath upward at the loose hair that hung over her brow. "Yes," she said.

"You should allow me," he said, moving his left hand out in an open gesture.

She shook her head. Then she looked at the cedar log and apparently changed her mind. "All right," she said, "but let me take care of your horse."

He could see perspiration on her face, and a few loose hairs stuck to the sides of her cheeks below the temples. He looked at her hands, which looked too small and pretty to be handling an ax. Then he followed her glance to the house, where Sam sat with his back to the foundation.

"Say hello to Mr. Quinn, Sam."

The little boy looked up and said, "Hi."

Quinn gave him a serious nod. "Hello, Sam."

135

Marie carried the ax, head down, and set it in front of Quinn. "I hate to give up," she said, "but this one has got me beat. I can cut the others, in my own good time, but this one's too hard."

"I'll give it a try," he said, handing her the reins and taking the end of the ax handle.

He noticed that the thick part of the haft, where it entered the head of the ax, was bruised and splintered. He lifted the ax and ran his thumb across the edge of the blade; it felt dull. He said nothing and went to where the length of wood lay on the ground.

He swung hard and fast, pulling sharply on the downstroke, and he made small chips fly. After he had notched the log all the way around, he turned the ax head around and gave a hard blow with the flat side. The log buckled, and then with another stroke of the blade he popped the stove length free. In similar fashion he cut through the log two more times to produce three more lengths of firewood. When he was done, he was breathing hard.

Marie had been watching without saying a word. "I feel better now, seeing how much trouble it was for you."

His chest heaved as he took deep breaths. "That log was a hard one," he said. "It should burn good." He helped her pick up the four pieces and then followed her to the shed in back of the house, where they stored the firewood and the ax.

Quinn surmised that she must have slipped into the house after putting his horse in the corral, for her hair was combed and retied. After she closed the door of the shed, she said she was making coffee. She went back into the house, and Quinn turned his attention to Sam.

"Do you know what cedar smells like, Sam?"

The little boy shook his head.

"Well, I'll show you." Quinn knelt and picked up a few of the pink and white chips he had nicked off the log. He carried the handful over to Sam and knelt again. "This is cedar. It's a kind of tree. When it dies, it makes good firewood. And it has a pretty smell." He held the handful of chips under the boy's nose. "Smells good, doesn't it?"

The boy turned his head aside and nodded.

Quinn stood up, stepped back, and dropped the chips. He heard the back door open, and a minute later he saw Marie carrying the pewter tray. This time it had cookies as well as two cups of coffee.

"It's actually rather pleasant here in the sun," she said. "Let me go get our stools." She handed him the tray and walked back to the stable.

When they were seated, she seemed to have regained all of her composure. "Well," she said, "have you finished roundup?"

"Yes, we have. Sully has a little more work for me, and then I'm off."

Her eyebrows rose a little. "Where to?"

"Oh," he said. "I mean I'm off work. I don't have any plans to go any place yet."

"Oh," she said, nodding. "I thought maybe you had some place to go, or . . ." Her voice trailed off.

Quinn took up the slack. "Not really. At one

time I might have had someone to go see, but that's in the past."

Her eyes lowered. "I didn't mean to be inquisitive."

"Not at all," he said, trying to make it sound cheerful.

She raised her eyes to meet his. "You haven't talked much about your past. Of course, maybe I haven't given you much of a chance, since I've talked so much about myself."

Quinn pushed out his lower lip and brought it in. "If I haven't talked much about my past, it's because there's not much to talk about. I've worked. And I met a girl I knew for a little while. And then I worked some more." He glanced at Sam and then back at Marie. "I did have one little bit of trouble that I could tell you about, just to be telling you a true story." He felt himself smiling easily.

"It's not bad, then?" Her eyes had picked up some sparkle.

"Oh, I wouldn't say so. It was just a bad time I went through, and I'd say it's all wrapped up and put away. But it makes a story." He smiled again and sipped on his coffee.

"Oh, good," she said, laughing lightly. "It's refreshing to hear that someone else has had trouble."

They drank coffee and ate cookies as he told the story of the Six Pines Ranch and how poor it had made him feel. At the end he said, "When you get dragged through something like that, you feel cheap, even though you know it wasn't your fault." He paused and then went on. "And yet you feel like some of it was your fault, because you didn't fight back. You let 'em get away with it, and then you go off bitter and blame yourself."

Marie wrinkled her nose and shook her head. "You can't change people like that. I think you did the best thing by getting out, without making any more trouble."

"That's what I tell myself. After all, who wants to get in with an outfit that doesn't trust its help? And what's the good of fightin' 'em about it? When you're fired, you're fired. Go work someplace where you can hold your head up." He took a deliberate breath and then continued. "I'll say that for Sully. He might work you into the ground, but you don't ever feel he doesn't trust you."

"That's good," she said. After a moment's pause she spoke again. "What kind of work does he have in mind for you?"

Quinn laughed. "I don't know. This fella I work with, Newman, he says the boss gives you more of whatever you shine at. Newman ended up doin' a lot of ropin'. I imagine I'll end up cuttin' firewood."

She had a sparkle in her eyes as she smiled and said, "You do shine at that. But I've got a hunch you're a good cowhand, too."

He toyed with the handle of his coffee cup. "I think I am. What makes you think so?"

"Your boots," she said. "The tops of the toes are

worn. And whenever you come by here, you've never ridden your horse too hard."

"I didn't know women noticed things like that."

Her face had good color as she smiled in the October sunlight. "Some do."

Chapter Nine

Quinn looked out the bunkhouse door in the first gray light of morning. The leafless cottonwood tree stood lone and stark in the middle of the ranch yard, and the wagon beneath it looked somber. In a little while the sun would rise and brighten up the scene, bringing out the yellow of the fallen leaves and the painted green box of the wagon.

The cattle were up already, milling and lowing in the pasture where they were being held. Quinn could smell dust in the faint cool breeze. Sipe and Dexter would throw the steers in with the larger herd later in the day, and they would head north to the shipping point. Quinn, as he understood it now, would be heading south.

Sully wanted him to deliver a horse to Chugwater, one of the earlier cowtowns, which lay at a long ride south. Now that the days were shorter, the trip would take three full days. Dexter had worked with the horse all season, and Sully thought it had good promise as a competitive roping horse. The horse was in a class all by itself, he said, and he wanted to turn it over to an old friend down in Chugwater. The friend had a man who could refine it for some of the prize-money events in Cheyenne and other larger towns.

Quinn felt the weight of responsibility in the job he had been assigned. This common-looking brown horse with a white blaze and front white socks was, in Sully's eyes, the most valuable horse on the ranch, and Quinn was going to have it in his hands until he delivered it safely to Mr. George in Chugwater. Sully must have sensed Quinn's apprehension, for he told him not to fret. This was a workhorse, after all, he said. Quinn could switch off and ride him for part of the way each day.

Sully told Quinn that for his main mount, he should pick whatever horse he wanted from his string. Quinn understood he was to ride back with just one horse, so he picked a large sorrel he had ridden several times on roundup. He thought the horse had good stamina and would be the best for the trip.

He packed his gear carefully, knowing that it had to ride behind him on the saddle. He thought of packing his things on the brown horse, which would have been fine for the trip down, but then he would have an extra saddle or pack saddle to worry about. Since he had to travel light on the way back, he decided to do things the same in both directions.

In other circumstances he might have asked Sully if he could take his own horses and then be on his way after he delivered the horse, but he had the sense that Sully wanted to keep him employed through the end of his pay period after all, and riding a ranch horse back was wage work. Besides, Quinn did not have any interest in things to the south. Cheyenne was another day's ride beyond Chugwater, but Quinn felt nothing pulling him there. He had received a short note from Sarah when he was on roundup, and it had politely released him from any tacit agreements they might have had.

The ride back, then, figured as the more enjoyable part of the job. He would have taken care of his responsibility, and he would be on his way back to a part of the country where he would like to do more visiting.

The sun was coming up when Quinn rode out of the ranch yard, his warbag and bedroll tied to the back of his saddle, and the brown horse trotting bareback at the end of a lead rope.

The ride south went smoothly. Quinn rode right through Hartville without stopping, and he was glad to see no one he knew. Dusk was falling as he came out on the plain on the other side of town, and dark was closing in as he made camp on the river.

On the second day he came to the Laramie River and followed it west, crossing it at Uva. He rode on and camped at a small creek that evening, within view of a large irrigation ditch, dry now at the end of the season.

On the third day he rode into Chugwater in the late afternoon. Like most cowtowns in the region, it was quiet and dusty with few trees, all of them small. Quinn had been through the town before and had found it agreeable. It had come into being as a ranching community, had hosted a stage station on the old Cheyenne-to-Deadwood line, and had continued as an important stop on the Cheyenne and Northern Railroad. The tracks ran north and south along the east edge of town, parallel to the road Quinn was traveling.

Quinn stopped first at a livery stable, where he asked about Sully's friend, Mr. George. The stable keeper, an older man in a wool cap and wool jacket, explained that Mr. George was out of the area at present but was expecting a "trustworthy man" to deliver a fine horse. He stated further that Mr. George's foreman was in town at that very moment, relaxing in the saloon next door. The stable man offered to go tell him the horse had arrived.

Mr. George's foreman was apparently enjoying his relaxation, for he sent word back that Quinn could leave the horse at the stable and join him in the saloon. Once inside, Quinn was introduced to the man, who stood up from a table full of cow-punchers and said his name was Douglas.

This man was a few years older than Quinn, taller and a little thicker. He had dark, bushy side whiskers, full lips, and a set of clear brown eyes. He thanked Quinn for delivering the horse, and he said he had a gift from Mr. George, which he hoped Quinn could take back.

Quinn said it depended on the gift, as he had only one horse.

Douglas motioned to the barkeep, who brought over a bundle wrapped in a brown wool blanket. He set it on the bar next to Douglas, who untied the twine, unwrapped the wool blanket, and unfolded a piece of light blue cotton cloth. There, sitting on the bar, was a beautiful mantel clock. It was not very large—the face was about five inches in diameter—but it was obviously valuable. It had gold plating and sat cradled in a polished rosewood base.

"It weighs about five pounds," Douglas said.

Quinn slipped his hands underneath the blanket and lifted the clock and its wrappings. "I can do it," he said.

"Good," replied Douglas, who then rewrapped the bundle, tied the twine, and shook Quinn's hand.

Quinn imagined that Douglas was enjoying his visit in town, especially with his employer gone. The foreman cast his glance from time to time at the table where his companions were talking.

Douglas said he was in town for the evening, or else he would invite Quinn to stay the night at the ranch.

Quinn said it was all right, that he had already found a place to stay—which he had, in the sense that the liveryman had told him he could have a bunk for two bits if he wanted.

Douglas shook Quinn's hand again, wished him

a good trip home, and then went back to join the group of drinking companions.

Quinn carried the bundle back to the livery stable, where he set it in the straw and arranged to stable his own horse as well as himself for the night. As it was getting dark inside the barn, the stable man lit a lantern and hung it on a post near the cot he had pointed out. Quinn laid out his bedding, set the clock in its bundle next to his warbag, and sat on the edge of the bunk.

The stable man, having taken Quinn's money, sat on a wooden box and seemed inclined to make conversation. "Nice fella, that Douglas."

"Uh-huh."

"Not real big on buyin' drinks, though."

Quinn shrugged. "He seemed interested in getting back to his table of friends. But he was polite enough to me."

The stable man smiled and showed a mouth of spaced, yellow teeth. "Can't miss that gossip. That's what it looked like when I was in there. These boys that don't git to town very often, they hang on every word."

"I imagine."

"And of course, you git a good piece of news buzzin', and they got to turn over every little bit of it."

Quinn raised his eyebrows. "Oh. Did something happen?"

"Not really. There's just been a fella in town, hangin' 'round, askin' questions."

"Uh-huh."

The older man peered at Quinn with his pale

eyes set back in his weathered face. "He's lookin' for someone."

Quinn sniffed. "Maybe he'll find him."

The wool cap moved up and down in the lantern light. "He might."

Quinn began to take interest. "Where's he from?"

"Down south. I think he's a damn fool comin' up here this time of the year, but he seems bound and determined."

"Older man? Younger man?"

"Older. Older than you. Damn near my age."

"What's he got for a name?"

"Goes by Larkin."

Quinn shook his head. The name meant nothing. "Who's he lookin' for, or is he kind of secret about that?"

The old man shook his head. "Not secret at all. He says he's lookin' for a man named Pat Slade. Thinks he might be workin' in this country."

"Might be," said Quinn. "It's a big country, with men comin' and goin' at all different kinds of work."

"He's got a hunch that this here Slade is workin' on a ranch, so he's askin' for descriptions of every new hand that's come into the country."

Quinn let out a low whistle. "Half of 'em are leavin' about now."

"Yep."

Quinn smiled and rubbed his beard. "How do you know I'm not this fellow Slade, in disguise?"

The old man's smile halfway closed his eyes. "You got dark hair and I'd say hazel eyes. And I hope you don't mind my mentionin' it, but he didn't say nothin' about a hook nose. This here Slade is supposed to have brown hair, blue eyes, medium build, and he smokes cigarettes. That ain't you."

Quinn laughed. "No, but it's half the punchers in this country." He thought of the cowhands he had met. Sipe had blue eyes but smoked a pipe. Dexter rolled his own pills, as he called them, but he had green eyes. Cater was on the move, but he was above medium build and had blond hair. Now Newman . . . Quinn gave it a thought. "Where's this Slade come from?"

"Texas," said the old man, with a nod of the head. "West Texas."

"Amarillo?"

"This fellow Larkin isn't that specific. He just said west Texas. Why?"

Quinn gave his head a quick shake. If it was Newman, he didn't need to be setting a bloodhound on his trail. "I don't know. It's the only town I know of down there."

"There's a million towns down there, from El Paso to Naggidoches, and damn few of 'em worth knowin'."

"Uh-huh."

The old man drew a silver-plated watch from inside his coat. "It's past seven," he said. "I usually have a little nip about this time." He looked at Quinn.

Quinn reached into his pocket and brought out a silver dollar. "Do you think this could get us both a little nip?"

The old eyes lit up. "You bet. You wait right here, and I'll be back directly."

When the old man had settled onto his box again, after pouring a nip into each of two tin cups, Quinn returned to their earlier topic. "What did this Pat Slade do wrong?"

The stable man had his cup on his lap, surrounded by both hands. He leaned forward and said, "He turned on his partner."

"Double-crossed him?"

"Run off and left him." The old man sat back up straight. "The way the story goes, this fella Slade and his partner got into a shootin' scrape over some horses, and they went on the run. The other fella got shot up. Somewhere out there in west Texas, Slade took his horse and left him to die. Might even have finished him off, 'cause he had more than one bullet hole in him when they found him."

Quinn let out another low whistle. "What's Larkin got to do with it?"

"He's some kind of kin to the man that got shot up."

Quinn nodded. "Makes sense. He just wants to get even."

The old man lowered his lip and showed his yellow teeth as he nodded and said, "Damn even."

Early the next morning, while Quinn was brushing his horse, a man came into the stable. The man took no notice of Quinn but talked in a low voice with the stable man. The stranger had the appearance of being from somewhere else, so Quinn took a good look at him.

He was an older man, probably about fifty. He wore a dark, flat-crowned hat with a rattlesnake skin for a hatband. Below the hat, his dark hair, turning gray, covered his ears. His face carried a gray stubble, and his light brown eyes looked filmy in a yellow background. He stood in a slouch, with a dark wool overcoat covering his gunbelt. The coat was open in front, showing a narrow, protruding stomach that made his belt sag.

Quinn turned to lift his saddle blanket and pad, and when he turned back, the man was walking out of the stable.

"That's him," said the stable man in a low voice. "That's Larkin."

"Up early," said Quinn. He finished saddling the big sorrel, tied on his bedroll, warbag, and bundle, and took leave of the stable man.

"What's your name?" asked the old man as they shook hands.

"Quinn."

"Mine's Henley. Old Bob Henley. Good luck to you, Quinn."

"Thanks. And good luck to you."

Back on the trail north, Quinn decided he would travel straight north from Uva, rather than cut across to Hartville. He could follow the Platte as it turned north, and he could head back to the ranch from the southwest. As he had it mapped out in his mind he thought it might be a little shorter, and he could avoid going through Hartville.

The Laramie Mountains lay to his left all the

way, and in the afternoon he saw clouds building in the west. By the end of the first day he had crossed the Laramie River and was headed north. The sun broke through the clouds and shed slanting light on the plains just before it slipped behind the mountains, and then the world lay in dusk and shadow. Quinn looked to the west. Somewhere in those mountains, Newman and Blair were scouting for their upcoming expedition.

Newman up there, he thought. Off and on all day, Quinn had thought about Newman, wondering if he could be Pat Slade. He recalled Newman as he had first seen him, leading the horse with the empty saddle. It could be. Newman could have been working all this time at the Lockhart Ranch, smiling and staying out of trouble, trying to build up a little stake, and thinking about what might be coming up in back of him. Newman from Amarillo, where there weren't as many horse thieves as there used to be. It could be—if one of them got killed and the other hit the trail.

Light snow was beginning to fall when Quinn made camp. He decided to make a small tent out of his canvas ground sheet, draping it over a rope he ran north and south between two little cottonwoods. He had carried two ropes on this trip, so he ran the other one between two slightly larger trees about thirty feet apart. He used it as a picket line, tying the big sorrel by the lead rope he had used on the brown horse.

Back at his makeshift tent, Quinn stuffed the saddle into the north opening. The snow was coming down thicker now. He laid the blanket and pad on the ground inside, rolled out his bedroll, and covered it with the brown wool blanket he unwrapped from the clock. He was not as hungry as he was worried, so he decided to save his food for later. He set his hat and boots against the saddle, and with all his clothes on, including his coat, he crawled into his blankets.

He heard the wind whip up in the night, and twice he pushed up on his canvas roof in order to dislodge the snow. It was going to cover the ground, he thought, but it would take a lot to stop the big sorrel. That horse had a lot of heart.

He thought of Newman and Blair, up there in the mountains somewhere. They were probably not sitting around an open fire anymore, drinking whiskey, singing songs, and calling each other cousin. They were probably holed up good and close.

At the first faint light of morning, Quinn looked out the open end of his shelter but could see nothing. The wind was still blowing, and it had piled a drift at the end of his tent. The saddle was drifted over on its end as well.

A jolt of fear ran through him. A drift could be packed pretty tight. He was going to have to think about the predicament carefully. At times like this it could all come down to body heat, and he didn't want to lose any unnecessarily.

He found his hat and boots, shook them clean, and put them on. He could not sit up straight in his shelter, but he could lie on one side and arrange his things. He set the clock, now wrapped only in the smaller blue cloth, on the middle of his bed.

Crawling on one elbow, he poked his nose out the open end of his shelter. A crack of gray daylight showed where the wind had sculpted the drift away from the east corner of the opening. He could take off his hat and push his way out like a gopher.

If he did that, he thought, he was going to want to wipe off. He took the cotton cloth from around the clock and put it in his coat pocket. He looked at the clock, delicate and precious but worthless at the moment. He, Quinn, who never carried a watch, was trapped in a snowstorm where gold meant nothing and time was a matter of when the storm was over. The clock was stopped at a quarter after five, but even if it were still keeping time it would be useless. A shovel or an ax would be handy now, or a larger sheet of canvas—but he didn't have those things. He didn't even know if he still had a horse, but he knew he had better go out and see.

He pushed himself out into the open and stood up, then wiped himself off and put on his hat. The wind blew viciously. The first snow of the season was usually wet, but this one was dry and stinging as the wind drove it crosswise into his face. He shielded his eyes with his gloved left hand, and he was glad he had a beard.

The wind buffeted him as he walked up and over two drifts. He could see a few yards ahead of him, but he couldn't find the horse. He found the cottonwood tree and the rope—

His blood chilled at the sound of a deep neigh. There was the horse at the other end of the picket rope, a ghost horse half covered with ice, its back against a bush filled with snow. The dark eyes rolled as the horse whickered again. Quinn could see the shape of the horse now, though its upper half was crusted white and the lower half was a powdered shadow.

"Easy, boy," he said out loud. "We'll get out of this. It can't be this deep everywhere. We just have to wait for it to blow over."

He moved his right hand down the picket line, then his left hand up the lead rope to pat the crusted ridge above the horse's nose. "Easy, boy. Hang on." He patted the horse's jaw with the back of his gloved hand. "Just don't leave me. And don't die."

He knew there was nothing he could do for the horse until the storm was over. He could get them both lost, looking for a few blades of grass, but he wasn't likely to find any real feed. Guilt stung him inside as the wind and snowflakes stabbed him on the outside. He had always lived by the rule that a person shouldn't eat until he had taken care of his animals. But it was no use, and he was hungry now. So he crawled back into his shelter and ate from his cache of cold grub as he felt sorry for the horse.

All day he lay huddled in the low shelter, trying to conserve heat, as the wind blew without mercy. As daylight was starting to fade he went out again to check the horse, which neighed loudly but did not move from the cove of snow that had formed around it. The horse was trying to conserve heat, too, it looked like. The blanket of ice suggested that the horse's body had its own wisdom, and Quinn imagined the horse had eaten snow to satisfy its need for water.

Quinn thought it was still snowing, but he couldn't be sure, for all the snow was moving horizontally. He knew that the drifts were always worse where there was something to deflect the blowing snow, but he didn't know how much snow there was to begin with.

Back in his gloomy shelter, Quinn felt the anxiety closing in again. It would be a long night. He continued to push snow off the canvas above him, and he wondered how long the shelter itself would hold up. He also worried about the horse, that it would take off, or die at the end of its rope. He thought again of Newman and Blair, off in the mountains, and he told himself there was no point in worrying about them. He had enough to worry about right here.

Somewhere between midnight and dawn, the wind let up. It continued to blow, but not as fiercely as before. Quinn burrowed his way out of the shelter again and stood up. The wind was cold, but it was not stinging his face with brittle snowflakes. He could not see his footprints from the day before, and some of the drifts had grown noticeably higher. With dread in his heart, Quinn pushed through the snow to find the horse. Then he felt a surge of hope as he came to the spot. The sorrel horse was still standing in the same place, and it was alive. It snorted and neighed, but it let Quinn come near.

It took half the morning to brush the ice off the

horse, pack up the camp, coil the frozen ropes, saddle the horse, and tie on the load. Every motion was laborious, every step a major exertion of lifting one foot out of the snow and putting the other down in it. In some places the drifts were solid enough to stand on, but in most places his weight broke through.

Finally he had everything secure, so he set out on foot, leading the horse that had so much heart. Quinn looked back once at the little dent where his camp had been, and he shook his head. Then he looked ahead and concentrated on punching his way out of the wasteland of drifts and dunes. By now the sun had come out, though the wind was still frigid. Quinn walked onward, putting one foot in front of the other and leading the horse.

Twice in the day he saw coyotes—once a lone dog looking over its shoulder, and once a pair moving along about fifty yards apart. Hunting, he thought, as Sipe had said.

Toward late afternoon he saw higher ground to the east. Thinking that it might be blown off a little clearer, he led the horse up a slippery incline. His hunch proved worthwhile, for up on top there was little snow, and the winter-brown grass bent in the wind.

He picketed the horse to let it feed all night, and he made his camp on the bare ground. He laid the saddle on the ground for a windbreak, wrapped his bed with the canvas sheet, and crawled in for another cold night.

The next day broke fairer, with no wind. The sun warmed up, and the snow began to melt where it was thinnest. Quinn let the horse graze till mid-morning, and then he saddled up. He decided to see if the horse would carry him, and when he swung his foot over the saddle he half expected the horse to fold underneath him. But it didn't. The big sorrel picked up its feet and stepped out.

Late in the afternoon he came to the Platte. He decided to follow it on this side, as it looked as if quite a bit of snow had settled among the trees on the other side. No one had left tracks since the snow, but he knew it was a well-traveled trail. After he followed the river for about an hour, he saw an object ahead that didn't look right.

Drawing closer, he saw that it was a dead badger lying splayed out on top of a jagged stump. Someone had obviously shot it before the storm and laid it on the stump for the amusement of fellow travelers. The sorrel horse snorted and walked wide around the animal, and Quinn did not find it hard to look straight ahead.

That evening he made camp again, hoping it would be his last cold night out for a while. The world seemed better now, a little more benevolent, as the horse had grass to eat and the man had a fire to sit by. When the sun went down behind the mountain, the air chilled quickly. The moon came up, a bright half-moon on a clear night. Quinn took off his gloves and held his hands to the fire. All was quiet. He could hear the horse shifting its feet on the ground; then he heard the loud wail of a coyote, sounding like a cry of triumph as it lifted into the cold night air.

Chapter Ten

Quinn saw the lights of the ranch buildings from the top of the last little ridge going into the ranch. After being gone seven nights, and the last four of them in lonely, cold, dark conditions, he felt more gratification than he might have expected. The lights, few and dull though they were, meant warmth and security. Except for his campfires, Quinn had not seen a man-made light since the lantern in the stable in Chugwater. Although he usually did not feel an urgency to be in the company of other people, the lights now conveyed a sense of comfort. Down in those buildings there were people who could care if he froze to death.

He hoped that farther to the north, on the way to Lost Spring, there was another person who cared about his well-being. He had thought more about her on the way down than on the way back. In the last few days, as he was absorbed with the basic needs of covering ground and surviving, thoughts of a pretty woman in the sunlight had seemed remote, unrealistic—a luxury. Now as he saw the lights, he imagined there were lights in her windows as well.

During the past four days he had thought about Newman more than about Marie. Quinn had assumed Newman was battling the weather just as he had been. He had felt a sympathy, at least, for a man he thought was stranded in the mountains not too far across the cold country. Furthermore, the rumor he had heard in Chugwater had stuck to his ribs. He tried not to dwell on the idea, because he did not know if Newman really was Slade, and if so, whether Slade had been as treacherous as the story made him out to be. He knew he did care whether Newman was all right, and he wondered if his friend was still up in the cold, dark mountains or huddled in a warm building like those below.

Quinn rode the big sorrel down to the barn, stripped the gear, and rubbed down the horse. Then he turned the sorrel into a stall, where he dumped oats and pitched hay. The horse had pulled through just fine, and he was going to be all right.

Quinn left his saddle in the barn as usual. Carrying his other bundles, he crossed the yard to the bunkhouse. Inside, only Sully and Moose were seated at the table. Quinn left his personal things on his bunk and carried the bundle into the eating area.

Moose looked at him wide-eyed. "You look like you had it rough."

"I did. I got caught in the snowstorm." He set the bundle on the table in front of Sully.

"What's this?" asked the boss.

"A gift from your friend," Quinn answered. "I didn't get to meet him in person, but his foreman gave this to me."

Sully untied the twine and unwrapped the package carefully until he unveiled the clock. It looked just as it had looked on the bar in Chugwater, and it still read a quarter past five.

"That's beautiful," Sully said in a soft voice. He put his hands on the rosewood base and scooted the clock about an inch. "George is really a fine fellow." Then he looked up at Quinn, his wide-set eyes not as cold as they usually looked. "Thanks, Quinn. It looks as if this cost you a little grief."

Quinn shrugged. "I was coming back anyway."

Moose laughed, and Sully smiled and nodded.

Quinn went to clean up, and as he was looking at his haggard face in the mirror, Sully said good night and left with his parcel. Quinn went back to the mess table and sat down.

"What news?" he asked.

Moose looked at him with his mouth pursed

and his new mustache bristling out. "You haven't heard."

"No, I came across country. I haven't talked to anyone."

"Well, Newman and his partner Blair had it rough."

Quinn gave him a close look. "Really?"

"Yep. They got caught in a hell of a snowstorm. They went up there and set their camp, and when they thought the worst of the storm was past, they went out on horseback. Blair's horse took a spill into a canyon. They had to shoot the horse, and then they got Blair onto another horse and headed back down. Blair died on the way back."

Quinn felt himself sink in his chair. "He did. How about Newman?"

"I guess he came through it all right. He's down there at Blair's now, helpin' the missus."

Quinn let out a long breath. "Who did you hear this from?"

"Singletree rider. He delivered the mail today, and he was full of the story."

"I bet."

Quinn thought for a moment. "I guess I should go down there and help him."

Moose pushed a platter of meat and gravy toward him. "Tomorrow morning should be soon enough."

"Oh, yeh," said Quinn. "I should say so."

As he lay in his bunk that night, Quinn remembered how reassuring it had been to see the lights of the ranch. Now it was good to be in the comfort of the bunkhouse; but even more so, it was good to be in the company of people who cared about one another. Even Sully, in his reserved way, had shown some concern, and although only Sully and Moose had been in the bunkhouse, Quinn felt as if he had come home.

As he thought about how comforting it had been, in its small way, Quinn realized how far he had come since the Six Pines Ranch. That episode had been a disheartening experience, and now he realized it had been quite a while since he had anguished over it and felt the bitterness come back up like a bad taste. He knew that time itself had put the events at a distance, but he also thought that working at the Lockhart Ranch had been good medicine.

Newman's earliest account had proven true—Sully was dry but fair. As Quinn thought it over, he supposed Sully had gathered a thousand small impressions and formed his judgments carefully; but in the end it was apparent that he trusted Quinn and appreciated him. Quinn realized now that some of the faith he himself had lost had been restored.

It went hand in hand, he thought, with his prospects with women. His disillusionment with the toadies at the Six Pines had come at the same time as his disenchantment with Sarah. He had built back up from that letdown, also. Now he could remember the old feeling—not so old, really—of what it was like to be near a woman, to hear the rustle of her clothing, to see the contour of a cheekbone or the curve of a body, to smell soap and perfume, to feel the tingle in the air as she came close.

Life had been down in a boghole, and now he could look back and see that the bad part was behind. Naturally he could not see ahead and foretell what would come next, but he felt calm and optimistic. It really did seem once again as if a person could hope for decent work such as here at the Lockhart Ranch, where, even if the boss didn't show much affection for his men, he treated them with dignity. It seemed also that a fellow could hope again for the chance of getting to know a woman who cared about life in some of the same ways he did. If Marie turned out not to be that woman, at least she had helped renew his faith in what life might yet have to offer.

The next morning, after the comforts of hot water and soap, and with the go-ahead from Sully, Quinn set out toward Blair's place. He had not been there before, but he had a good idea of where it was and he found it without difficulty.

Mrs. Blair answered his knock on the door and invited him into the kitchen, where she and Newman had been drinking coffee. Quinn reflected that Newman had met her on two or three previous occasions and probably counted as a friend with her, and he sensed an easy atmosphere in the kitchen. He noticed that the housekeeping was casual, with items, including Newman's hat, piled on the end of the table. A large kettle sat at the back of the stove, with the handle of a wooden spoon sticking out of it. On the wall above the sideboard hung a set of mule deer antlers, four points on each side plus eye guards. A wool cap hung from one side of the antlers, and a leather strap hung from the other.

Quinn took a glance at Mrs. Blair as she found him a cup and poured him some coffee. The woman was relatively young, probably about thirty. She wore a loose-fitting gray cotton dress and a brown wool sweater over it, plus a pair of heavy shoes, but Quinn thought she might have a shape beneath it all. Her other features were common but not homely. Quinn noticed her shoulder-length, sandy-colored hair, which she kept brushing away from her cheekbones; he also took note of her pale face and pale blue eyes, her small chin, and her thin mouth. She looked harried, which Quinn thought was normal under the circumstances. Life with Blair had probably not been easy, and now she had grief.

Quinn learned that the body had been taken into town, which meant Hartville, and would be buried the next day.

Newman went on to explain that the hunting expedition was canceled but all the camp equipment was still up in the mountains. "We need to get that stuff back," he said. "It's worth something, and Mrs. Blair doesn't have much."

Quinn looked at her, and she gave him a blank look in return. He realized Newman had not stated specifically what he meant by "we," but he assumed his own help would be welcome. He offered, and Newman accepted.

Quinn decided he would use his own saddle horse and packhorse, so he offered to go back to the Lockhart and get them.

Newman said he could ride northwest out of Hartville after the funeral, and Quinn could ride southwest from the ranch, to meet on the river where it headed north. Newman said he had left Blair's other two packhorses at a ranch, and they could pick them up on the way.

Quinn agreed to the plan, and after finishing his coffee he said good-bye, leaving Newman and Mrs. Blair to tend to the sad affairs.

Quinn waited at the river for at least two hours, he supposed. The weather had not warmed back up, although much of the snow was melted in open areas. He walked up and down the flat stretch of river bottom, to stay warm and to work off his impatience.

Finally Newman came riding through the bare trees on a horse that Quinn recognized from Blair's string. Newman was wearing thick gloves and a long fur coat, and he had a large bedroll tied to the back of his saddle.

"Nice coat," said Quinn, as Newman drew rein.

"Yeh. I got it from Blair. He said he had it made from all the coons he trapped for two winters."

Quinn raised his eyebrows. It would be an expensive coat, and few working cowboys could afford it. He remembered Sipe's comment that Blair was going to stake Newman to a winter coat, and he had apparently done so.

"How's Mrs. Blair?" Quinn asked.

"As well as can be expected. A little down in the mouth, naturally. But she'll get through it." Newman adjusted his reins and then said, "She appreciates you lendin' a hand."

"Glad to be able to," Quinn answered.

They crossed the river and rode north, keeping to the higher ground, until Newman suggested they camp. The shadows were reaching out, and the men had a full day's ride ahead of them, anyway.

The campfire cheered things up when dusk set in. Quinn had packed the bare necessities on his packhorse, knowing there was a full camp waiting for them. He cut pieces of salt pork and set it frying in the skillet, and before long the smell of frying pork blended with the aroma of boiled coffee. Moose had sent some cold biscuits along, plus a little bag of dried apples. It was a good camp, cozy and cheerful, and Newman seemed in good spirits. Quinn thought he had come through the ordeal rather well.

At the same time, though, Quinn could not set aside the idea that the man he was with could be Pat Slade. Finally he thought of a way to bring it up. "Ever hear of a man named Larkin?"

Newman pressed the fingertips of his gloves

John D. Nesbitt

together and shook his head. "No, can't say that I have."

"Or Slade?"

Newman cocked his head. "There's some of them back home." He looked at Quinn. "In fact, there was one in your old home town of Julesburg, way back when. A real wolf of a feller, but I think they finally hung him up in Montana."

"Oh, yeh," said Quinn. "He's part of the legend. That all happened before I was born."

Newman looked back at the fire. "Why do you ask?"

Quinn looked at Newman, hunched into his fur coat. "Oh, just something I heard. Down in Chugwater. I heard there was a man named Larkin lookin' for a man named Slade." That would be enough, he thought. If Newman really was Slade, he could take warning. And if not, it was like smoke on the wind.

Newman made a squeaky sucking sound through his teeth. "There's always someone lookin' for someone else."

Quinn didn't have an answer, so he just nodded as he poked some of the unburned ends into the fire.

Morning broke clear and chilly. Newman got a big fire going and soon had a bed of coals for coffee and breakfast. The sun had barely cleared the eastern hills when the two men broke camp and headed back out onto the trail. They rode north a ways farther and then turned west to follow a creek through a little valley and up toward the mountains.

168

"Up ahead where this valley narrows," Newman said, "we'll pick up them other horses."

They made their stop and then rode on through the afternoon with a string of three extra horses. They went through bare foothills and across sagebrush flats, gently climbing all the way, until they came to a place where the mountains rose abruptly and the creek came tumbling out of a steep rock canyon.

Newman pointed to the right. "Up in there. About another hour or so."

Snow lay on the ground nearly everywhere, with only a few open spaces clear. Quinn saw a little grass, but not much. As the horses climbed up into the rugged country, shadows stretched out from the dark timber and the air was chilly.

"We'll get there with not much time to spare, it looks like," Quinn said. He looked at Newman, who seemed nonchalant in his heavy coat and gloves.

Newman nodded without looking around. "Just right," he said.

They reached the camp just before the sun dropped behind the high ridges. Quinn looked over the camp, and he thought Blair had done a good job of setting it up. Two wall tents, about ten by twelve, stood side by side. The one on the left had a canvas fly stretching out as an awning. It sagged with snow. To the right side of the fly was the fire pit, and behind the pit sat a pile of dry branches ready to be broken up into firewood.

"We've got grain," said Newman. "We can feed

these horses right now and put them on a picket line. Then we can stop and let 'em graze down on the bottom tomorrow." He looked at Quinn and nodded. "Feed 'em in the mornin', too, of course."

They stowed their gear in the tent on the left, and Newman made a big fire again. He tossed on whole branches and let them burn through, then flipped the two and three-foot ends into the fire.

All this time, Quinn was troubled with the idea that Newman might be Slade, but he did not feel he had the level of confidence to bring up the subject again. From time to time he took a look at Newman, sitting in the firelight in his hat and coat and gloves. Newman did not seem troubled—indeed, he seemed cozy in the coat he might not have to pay for—and he said very little about Blair.

Quinn looked at the blaze and remembered thinking about the two men up here, wondering if they were drinking and singing by the campfire. Now Blair was gone, just like that, and here they were, rounding up his effects.

In the morning after breakfast, Newman said he could use a hand getting a rope he had left back in the trees. Quinn followed him between the tents and back into a stand of pine trees, where they came to a hanging carcass. Quinn could tell it was a deer, though it had been skinned, and rather neatly at that. The backstraps had been cut out on either side of the backbone, but the rest of the meat was still on the carcass. The front and hind quarters looked as if they

were in good shape, as the bullet hole and blood-
shot meat were down on the brisket where the
heart and lungs would have been. Quinn thought
the meat was aged just about right, and he was
surprised that all Newman had mentioned was
the rope.

"Nice deer," he said.

"Uh-huh," Newman answered. "If you lift 'er
up, I'll untie it."

The carcass was dry as well as cold to the
touch, having cased up well in the weather.
Quinn lifted the deer by its front end, and the rear
hocks went straight up above him and gave
Newman the slack he needed.

Quinn stood with the stiff deer upside down in
his arms, wondering where he might set it, when
Newman said, "Just toss it on the ground."

Quinn looked around. "You don't want to save
any of it?"

"Nah. We got ten days' worth of grub without it."

Quinn dropped the carcass in the snow, where
the hind quarters bounced and then lay still. As
he leaned over to untie the rope from the ham-
strings, he told himself it wasn't his camp. Saying
nothing more, he went back to the clearing to
help Newman strike the tents.

It took most of the morning to get the camp
folded up, rolled up, and packed. The horses were
loaded heavily, and there was less grub and grain
than before. Quinn reviewed the details he had
heard. If Blair's horse had been shot and he rode
out on what had been a packhorse coming in, and

Quinn replaced it with his own packhorse, the horses must have been unbelievably loaded down.

"Did you have only three packhorses coming in?"

"No," said Newman, in his casual tone of voice. "We had four."

"What happened to the other one?"

"Blair took it up the canyon and shot it. For bear bait. It was a pretty poor horse anyway."

They came down off the mountain slowly, leaving the dark timber behind as the shadows were starting to lengthen. Down on the flat, they camped along the creek they had followed on the way in. After building a fire, they sat with their backs against a screen of chokecherry trees. The stream was down to a trickle at this time of the year, and iced at the edges, but it made an audible sound. The horses grazed on their pickets, their hooves crunching the dry leaves that had fallen from the chokecherry and box elder trees. All in all it was a peaceful setting, and Quinn thought a newcomer would not have guessed the fury this area had seen a few days earlier.

"What do you think Mrs. Blair will do?" he asked.

Newman had taken off his gloves to roll a cigarette. "Probably sell out."

"Really?"

"Oh, yeh. All these ranchers like to pick up homesteads when they can."

Quinn nodded. It gave them more water to control, and so it extended their range. "Who do you think would be interested in it?"

Newman licked the edge of his cigarette paper. "I believe she was gonna go talk to Sully, or have him come talk to her."

Chapter Eleven

Quinn watched Newman ride away through the trees in the river bottom. The trees, all leafless now, cast thin shadows on the lead rider and the string of packhorses. Newman had said he would take everything back to Blair's by himself while Quinn went to see if there was any word from Sully. Quinn, who had not had a great fondness for Blair when the man was alive, did not mind being relieved of the rest of the task of tending to his effects.

It was early afternoon on the second day after they had camped at the foot of the mountain. The temperature had climbed above freezing each day, and this day's temperature had turned out hospitable. Newman had taken off the heavier fur coat and had put on his blanket-lined canvas

174

coat, so Quinn saw the tan patch of color as Newman moved off through the trees.

Quinn arrived at the Lockhart Ranch at dusk, having enjoyed a sunset of crimson and orange that cast a rich glow on the dry plains. Now the sunlight was fading as he rode into the ranch yard, put his horse away, and carried his personal gear to the bunkhouse. He had been aware that today was the first of November, and he assumed he was off the payroll. He knew he was still free to stay as long as he wanted, but his obligations were up.

At the bunkhouse he learned from Moose that Dexter and Sipe had returned from shipping beef and were out checking cattle. They should be in before long, he said.

Quinn took the opportunity to get cleaned up and to put on clothes that didn't smell like campfire. Scrubbed and clean, he felt like a man of leisure when Sipe, Dexter, and Sully came in for supper.

The meal got under way without much talk until Sully set his knife and fork on his plate and pushed it a couple of inches forward. "Quinn," he said, "I've got a little more work for you if you want it. I've arranged to buy out Mrs. Blair, and I'd like you and Newman to get a tally for me."

Quinn looked at his plate and then across the table at Sully. "I can do that."

"Good. I told Mrs. Blair I thought you would. She said Newman would be coming back to her place, so I told her I would send you down there

175

if I could. She seems anxious to get out of here before winter if she can, and I don't blame her. Meanwhile, I can take care of transferring the deed and the brand."

"Sure."

Sully's eyes seemed to look at Quinn more directly now. "Get a full count of everything, and keep track of cows, calves, heifers, steers, and bulls—how many of each. And horses, too. I understand he's got those in a fenced pasture, so they'll be all right for the time being. As for the cattle, we'll get another count in the spring, but I want this to be as close as we can get it. I doubt we'll come out long over the winter, but if we do, I can make a back payment."

Quinn nodded and felt a small flush of pride. Sully was placing more confidence in him. "I'll tell Newman," he said. Then he paused, not knowing how to put what he wanted to say next. He had already had it in his mind that he was free to go visiting, and he didn't like to have to give it up. "There is one thing, though," he said.

"What's that?" The lantern light reflected in the dent of Sully's nose.

"I was wondering if I might have a little time off—maybe half a day—before I go over there."

Sully took a drink of coffee and looked up. "That'll be all right. But get there before it gets too late in the day tomorrow."

"Good enough. I will. And thanks."

Sully stood up and finished off his cup of coffee. "Thanks to you, Quinn," he said. Then he took his utensils to the dishpan, collected his hat, and left.

The mood cheered up as soon as Sully was gone. Sipe and Dexter had enjoyed themselves after delivering the beef herd, and they had bought all their winter clothing before they spent their money loosely.

Among the items Sipe had bought for the winter was a rifle scabbard, so he could hunt varmints through the winter. "Nice-smellin' new leather," he said. "Almost hate to take it out and get it beat up."

As a matter of casual conversation, Quinn asked Sipe what way he carried a scabbard, as there were different ways of tying one to a saddle. Some men tied it on in the northwest, or in front of the left leg; some put it on the southeast, behind the right leg; and some put it horizontally under a stirrup fender.

Sipe gave his head an exaggerated weave from side to side and said, "Ah do it the Arkansaw way."

Dexter laughed.

Quinn raised his eyebrows and looked at each of them, as if inviting an explanation.

Dexter began. "We met these two drovers from Arkansas in a saloon there in Chadron. They'd worked the whole season together on a ranch and had just brought the herd in, and they were ready to go home. One of 'em said he was lookin' forward to roastin' a pig when he got back to God's country. So Jeff here asks him how he kills his pigs, and he says 'the Arkansaw way.' His partner agrees. So Sipe asks what that was. The fellow goes on to explain that you stick 'em with a long knife, 'wot we call an Arkansaw toothpick,' and you stick it right in the throat below the jaw. You poke it clean through to the other side and you cut straight down, and there you are. Bleeds like a gusher."

Sipe was laughing. "Then his buddy says, 'No, that's not the Arkansaw way.' He goes on to say to stick 'em straight on, in the throat, right above the collarbone, where the main blood vessels meet. You twist the knife a couple of different ways on the way out, and it bleeds like a real stuck pig."

"I think either way would get the job done," said Moose. "But if you know how to do it, I'd guess the second way is better. It's the one I've heard of the most."

After a general round of agreement on that point, Quinn said, "Not bein' a hog man myself, I've always wondered how they scrape the hair."

"Oh," said Moose, "some of 'em pour boilin' water on the body and scrape it part by part, and others dunk it whole to scald it."

"The Arkansaw way," said Sipe, and everyone laughed. "Actually," he said, "they never got that far as long as we was there. But after that, me 'n' Jimmy went to a parlor, and we met a couple of nice little blond gals with pretty ankles, and we had plenty of jokes about how to do it the Arkansaw way."

Moose turned to Quinn. "You can tell when

these fellows have had their wick trimmed. They're just happy as hell."

The conversation went on to other topics, and before long it came around to a topic that made Quinn pay close attention. The man named Larkin had made his way to Hartville and was making inquiries there, and the news had found its way to Moose's cookshack, where Sipe and Dexter had had a chance to hear it also.

Sipe pushed himself back from the table and began reaming his pipe with his pocketknife. "Seems like lookin' for a needle in a haystack, if you ask me."

Dexter spoke up. "Especially if he's on this fellow's trail an' he goes around tellin' everyone who he's lookin' for."

Quinn, who had already given the idea quite a bit of thought, said, "He probably had to give some name. If he acted too secret, nobody would tell him anything. If he's got to give a name he might as well give the real one, because it might get him somewhere."

"Still," said Sipe, "I'd think it would send this Slade fellow right underground, soon as he heard it."

Dexter took out the makin's. "You never know. I think I'd cut and run, but then maybe I'd just as soon wait and have it out. You can't really know unless you're in it yourself."

"That's true," said Quinn. "And all anyone has heard, I imagine, is what this fellow Larkin says. If there is a Slade, you don't know his side of the story."

"I agree," said Moose. "From the way I heard the story, this here Larkin is plumb certain he's justified. But he might be too full of his own story, like a poisoned pup."

"Where's he from, anyway?" asked Sipe.

"I heard Louisiana," Moose answered. "The dead partner—Slade's partner—was named Corbeau, and that's the type of name that comes from down there."

Sipe came right back with his next question. "What's this Larkin look like?"

Moose pulled on his mustache. "I don't know."

"I saw him in Chugwater," Quinn said.

The others looked at him, and Dexter asked, "So you heard all this before?"

"Some of it. But like I said, I think it's a good idea to hold off on makin' judgments till you know the whole story—or as much of it as you're goin' to get."

There was a moment of quiet until Sipe asked, "Well, what's he look like?"

Quinn looked around at the other three, who were looking at him. "He's older—in his fifties, I'd say. He looks like he's from somewhere else." He nodded at Moose. "And he looks like poison."

Quinn made good use of his morning's liberty. His own horse deserved a rest after the trip to the mountains, and since Quinn was back on the payroll, he roped out the bay horse from his string and saddled it for his ride. He left the ranch shortly after sunrise, and the day was starting out a pleasant one. A red sky gave way to yellow above the hills to the east, and then daylight flooded the plains. It was the kind of moment that made him feel that life was still full of rich possibilities and that this part of the world at least was a good place to be. He had had a milder version of that feeling during the sunset the evening before, but now that he was on his way to visit Marie, he felt it more strongly.

The day did not lose its magic as the sunlight came over the country more thoroughly, but Quinn now saw the land in more actual detail. The grass was thoroughly dry by now, after a few weeks of frost and one real storm. The snow had all melted except in the darkest north-facing nooks, and the country had the general hue of late fall. Life had drawn back in to lie low in the roots of the buffalo grass, the chokecherry bushes, and the larger trees. The country gave a person the feeling that it was getting ready for winter.

Antelope were bunching into larger herds now, and the deer, what few there were, would be out feeding to store up fat against the winter. The snakes were already denned up, and the gophers had thrown up fresh dirt as they were digging in, too.

The wood shingles on Marie's roof gave a pale shine as Quinn topped the last rise going into her place, and a thread of smoke was rising from her stovepipe. He rode on into her yard, and as he drew up opposite the kitchen door, she stepped outside. He felt his pulse quicken.

She was wearing a plain blue sweater over a gray cotton dress, but she looked fine to him.

"Hello," she said.

"Good morning. Did I come at a convenient time?"

"Very convenient," she said, smiling. "Sam and I are baking cookies, and I was about to bring in more firewood."

"Let me put my horse up," he said, "and I'll be glad to fetch some."

"It's probably warmer right now in the corral anyway," she said, glancing around. "I was going to tell you to put him in the stable. That's where mine are."

"Corral's fine."

He left the saddle on and tied the horse, as usual. Then he went to the shed for an armful of wood. She opened the door as he came up the steps.

As it was the first time he had been in her house, he took a quick glance around before he went out for more wood. It was a neat, snug kitchen with an oak china cabinet and matching sideboard. The table was covered with baking ingredients and a large bowl of dough, and Sam stood on a chair at the far end of the table.

"Hello, Sam," he said.

"Hi."

Quinn brought in two more armloads of firewood and stacked it in the wood box. Then he took off his hat and coat and sat at the table where Marie indicated. She offered him a cup of coffee, which he accepted. He sipped on it slowly as she rolled dough and talked about recent events.

The storm had not hit very hard at her place,

she said. She understood it had been stronger down south and closer to the mountains.

He told of his trip to Chugwater and his ordeal on the way back.

"It sounds as if you were lucky," she said.

"I'd say so," he answered. Then he went on to tell her about Blair's coming to grief.

Marie paused in her work. "That's too bad. I feel sorry for Mrs. Blair. I've never met either of them, but I heard of him, of course, and I feel for her." Her dark eyes met Quinn's. "Losing a husband in this country is difficult for a woman, even if the husband was a hard man."

Quinn cleared his throat and said, "Sure seems like it."

"Do you know what she plans to do? I mean, will she stay here, with winter just coming on?"

Quinn watched the heels of her hands give smooth, forceful pressure to the rolling pin handles. "I don't think so. She's arranged to sell everything to Sully, and I understand she wants to get out before the real bad weather sets in."

"I see. Did Sully buy the land and the livestock both?"

"As I understand it. In fact, I'm supposed to go on down there later in the day and start makin' a tally for him."

"Oh." She rested the rolling pin for a second. "Then you're still working for him."

Quinn thought her comment suggested she was keeping track of the time, too. He registered that as a good sign as he gave his answer. "I thought I was off, but he put me back on. For this little job."

"That's good." She looked at him, and their eyes met. "I guess."

"Oh, yeh," he said. "I was in no hurry to go anywhere else, and I can always use a little more in the way of wages." As she turned back to her work he said, "How about you? Are you just about dug in for the winter?"

"Pretty close." She lifted a corner of the dough. "I wish I had a little more firewood, but you know what they say about wishes." She pinched off a piece of dough and fed it to Sam, who was still standing in his chair and watching.

Quinn felt as if he had to complete what she had begun. "If wishes were horses, all beggars would ride." Then he added, "I'd be happy to drag in a few more snags, if you'll tell me where to go to find them."

She laid her left hand on his right forearm. He could feel the light weight of her hand through the sleeve of his shirt. Then the hand lifted away.

"Oh, no," she said. "You're only going to be here a short while, and you're going to have to visit a little more."

"Good enough. But that'll give me an excuse to come back, to help you lay in more firewood."

"That would be all right, too," she said. She raised her left hand to brush hair away from her cheek, and her eyes sparkled as she smiled at him.

She started cutting out the cookies and putting them on a cookie sheet. Quinn watched in silence for several minutes until a thought came to him.

"I've been thinkin'," he said, "about something you said a while back."

She glanced at him and said, "Yes. What was it?"

"Well, I believe you said that when you marry a person, you find out if there's any trust."

She drew her lips together and nodded. "Yes, I think that's what I said."

He let out a breath. "Well, I wonder if you meant you have to marry a person to know that—to know there's something big missing."

She looked at him. "Well, no—I guess it depends."

He knew he had wanted to say what he said next. "Because, there was this girl I knew, and I thought I wanted to marry her, but before I ever got that far I knew it was no go."

"You mean there wasn't any trust?"

"It didn't even get that far. But I could tell there wasn't what there was supposed to be. Call it trust, or call it confidence, or whatever. I could tell we just didn't know each other in the right way—to know what made the other person tick."

Marie had paused in her work and now gave him a thoughtful look. "You were probably lucky," she said. "I agree that you don't necessarily have to marry someone to find out, but to go back to what I originally said—if there isn't any trust and you didn't know it before, you'll sure find out afterwards." She hesitated for a second and then said, "I don't want to sound like an expert, but I've been through my own travail, and I've done some observing since then as well."

Quinn smiled. "I have faith in your judgment. Now, that brings me to my second question. How about if there *is* trust? You don't have to marry someone to know that, do you?"

She gave a light, almost nervous, laugh. "Well, no. You could get this thing going around and around, to see which is the cart and which is the horse. Do you have to marry someone to know if there's the necessary trust? And how do you know what's necessary until you've been married?" She shook her head. "But there are degrees of trust. You can sense, early on, whether there's the basic kind." She blushed and did not look at him as she spoke. "Like between you and me, which I imagine is what you're hinting at. In our case, I could tell right away that we naturally understood one another."

Quinn felt a flush come to his own face. "I thought so, too. And I thought I could tell by comparing it with something that wasn't, if you know what I mean."

She looked at him now and nodded.

"I don't mean to be getting ahead of things," he said, giving her what he hoped was a knowing look, "but just speaking generally, I think you ought to be able to know some things without going all the way through."

"Well, I'm not sure what you mean by *know*, because you can't see ahead, but I'd agree you can form a pretty good idea." She shook her head. "Sadly, though, I think a lot of people go all the way through, as you say, until they find out what they wish they had known earlier. I know I did."

"But it doesn't have to be that way."

"No, I don't think so. At least I sure hope not. I hope we learn something as we go through these things."

Chapter Twelve

Quinn found Newman and Mrs. Blair once again at the kitchen table, drinking coffee. The table and sideboard had been tidied up somewhat, and Newman's hat hung from the deer antlers above the sideboard. Mrs. Blair herself looked a little better than the last time— less pinched and worried—although she was dressed about the same, in her loose and drab style.

After Quinn had explained the few details of Sully's instructions, Newman asked him if he had brought horses for the work.

"No," Quinn answered. "I assumed we would use these horses, since they're Sully's now."

"All the same to me." Newman rose from the table, took his hat from the deer antlers, exchanged a look with Mrs. Blair, and then stopped, halfway turned, with his hat in his hand. "Did you want some coffee, Quinn?"

"Oh, no. I'd just as soon get to work."

Quinn kept the tally as he and Newman counted stock. That afternoon they made one ride east of the ranch and met back at the corral at sundown. The days were still getting shorter, and the air chilled quickly as soon as the sun went down. Quinn jotted down the figures without pause, to catch the last of the fading light and to get the horses put away before complete darkness fell.

Although the weather was chilly, it was not as cold as it was in the mountains. Quinn had told Newman more than once that it was best not to wear the warmest clothes too soon. For one thing, as he explained, a person's body didn't work hard enough to produce heat. For another, if a fellow put on his warmest coat at ten below, he didn't have anything better to put on if the temperature dropped to thirty or forty below. Newman had taken the advice when they came down out of the mountains, and now he was still wearing the tan canvas coat, presumably saving the fur coat for the truly cold weather.

As evening drew in, the two men put away the horses and checked on the other stock. Then they went into the warm house, where supper was waiting. Mrs. Blair served fried chicken, boiled potatoes, and gravy. As she explained, she wasn't going to take the chickens with her, and Sully wasn't very interested in them. So she had dressed two chickens that afternoon while the men were out.

"T. John could eat a whole chicken by himself if he was left to it," she said. "So I didn't think two of them would be too much."

Quinn said very little during the meal. It was good-tasting food and a welcome change from the trail grub and bunkhouse meals he had been eating. He complimented Mrs. Blair on the food and thanked her.

Newman had pushed his chair back from the table and was rolling a cigarette, and Mrs. Blair was clearing the table. She had a dishpan of water on the stove, so she was apparently getting ready to wash dishes. She paused at Newman's place, and he looked up at her.

"Oh, yeh," he said. "That was a fine supper. Thanks."

Mrs. Blair nodded, took his plate, and turned to wash the dishes.

Newman had seemed to be in a good mood all afternoon, and indeed the whole atmosphere in the Blair household seemed much less gloomy than it had on Quinn's first visit. Now, as he rolled his cigarette, Newman was making jokes about how a man could make a great fortune in this country—buy a sheep ranch, hire a few Mexican sheepherders to do all the work, build a big mansion like the rich Englishmen did, and hire a cook from France.

"No Chinaman cook for me," he said, lighting the cigarette. "I don't like the way they make the bread."

Quinn laughed.

Mrs. Blair glanced over her shoulder. "I've heard they do it to the soup, too."

Newman blew a double stream of smoke through his nostrils. "I'll have to be on the lookout for them. The railroad camps and minin' camps have always been full of 'em, and the farther west you go, the more of 'em you find in the bunkhouse kitchens."

"Have you been out that way before?" Quinn asked.

"Nah, that's mainly what I heard."

The evening wore on in good-natured small talk, with Mrs. Blair coming in and out of the kitchen. When it was bedtime, she said the two men could sleep in the front room.

"I'll build up a good fire in the kitchen stove, and if you leave the doors open between rooms, the heat spreads out pretty well."

Quinn thought she was using up the firewood as liberally as she was going through the chickens, which was all right for him. He had noticed she had the doors open to her bedroom, the spare room across the hall from it, and the front room, which lay at the other end of the hall from the kitchen. When he went to the front room to roll out his bedroll on one of the two pallets she had put on the floor, he appreciated the relative warmth of the room. It was much more comfortable than a lot of sleeping rooms he had occupied.

He slept soundly, unaware of his surroundings. When he awoke, the room was dark, but a dull light showed from the other end of the hallway. He could hear movement in the kitchen, and he pictured Mrs. Blair building up the fire and putting on the coffeepot. He listened deliberately then, and he could hear Newman's even breathing on the other pallet.

The room was chilly by now, but Quinn knew it was much warmer than if he had slept out on the ground. He rolled out of his bed, got dressed, put on his hat and coat, and went outside. When he came back in, Newman was getting up. Quinn waited until Newman had made his trip outside, and then the two of them went to the kitchen together.

Mrs. Blair served up a breakfast of bacon, fried potatoes, and coffee. The men ate without wasting much time and then got ready for work, putting on their hats and coats and gloves. When they went out into the cold morning it was daylight, and Quinn could see heavy frost on the ground and on the corral poles. The men had brought their ropes inside the evening before, and Quinn now carried his beneath his coat to keep it limber for roping out his workhorse.

Newman pointed out the two horses he thought they could ride that morning, and in a few minutes the men were leading the two horses from the corral. Blair had a low stable for tack but no place inside for saddling horses, so they tied the horses to a hitching rail outside and did their work there.

Quinn's horse, a big bay, blew up its girth against the cinch, as a lot of horses did, so he walked the horse around a little before he retightened the cinch and climbed on. Before he even got his right foot into the stirrup, the horse went into bucking.

Quinn dug his spurs in and tucked his chin against his chest, and with both hands trying to shorten the reins and keep the horse from putting its head between its front feet, he concentrated on trying to keep his balance. The horse kicked up its hindquarters, came down, reared up with its front feet off the ground, came down hard, turned to the left, whipped to the right, went straight up, and came down on all fours in a jolt.

Quinn lost his hat as well as the right stirrup, but he dug in and held on. Usually a horse would buck itself out and then settle down for the rest of the day, but this one kept going—pitching, turning, and jolting. The horse wheezed and squealed and farted; the saddle leather flopped and squeaked; the ground and the corral rails and the stable went up and down and around as Quinn hung on.

He was choking Lizzie now—grabbing the saddle horn—and trying to decide whether to ride it out or bail off. Then Newman on his horse came crowding in on the left.

"Pile off," he hollered.

Quinn kicked loose of his one stirrup and let go

of the reins and pommel, leaned into Newman and the other horse, and grabbed Newman around the upper body. Then the two horses separated, Quinn's with a high kick that sprayed dirt but did no damage.

Newman brought his horse to a stop as Quinn let loose and slid to the ground.

"Sonofabitch really blew up, didn't he?" said Newman, who was reaching forward to take down his rope where he had tied it against his saddle. The bucking horse was still pitching, but it could level out at any time and head for open country. Newman spurred his horse forward as he brought up his rope and shook out his loop.

He came up behind the bay horse on its left just as it spurted away, but his horse was already in motion and picked up speed fast. Newman swung the loop a few times and then threw it out over the head of the runaway horse. Then, although he was a hard-and-fast roper, he dallied his rope around his saddle horn, as he had not tied it down ahead of time. He took a couple of dallies and turned his own horse to the left, and after making a wide turn he brought the rebellious horse back to the ranch yard.

"Do you want to try him again?" he asked Quinn.

The old rule was that a man just got back on, so Quinn said, "Sure." He gathered up the reins, loosened Newman's rope, and slipped it off. "Thanks," he said, smiling.

Newman was smiling, too. "We don't have to

spend all day at this. If he does it again, we can trade him in." Then he added, "Nice ride."

"Thanks." Quinn climbed on again, half expecting the horse to go back into action, but it just shivered once and waited for the rider's cues.

The two men covered quite a bit of ground that day, meeting at appointed times to compare counts and enter the tally. By the end of the day, Quinn had the impression that Newman was fudging the count in Mrs. Blair's favor. He decided to wait another day before he said anything.

On the second full day of work he paid close attention and even double-checked a couple of draws Newman had ridden down, and he was convinced Newman was padding the ledger.

Because Sully had put him in charge of the tally, Quinn felt responsible for coming out with an accurate count. He recalled Sully's remark that they probably would not come out long over the winter. Quinn certainly didn't want to come out too short, either. Finally he decided to mention it as he and Newman were riding in from the day's work.

"How close are your counts?" he asked.

"Oh, I don't know. Pretty close. Why?"

"Seems like yours might be a little generous at times."

Newman looked down and adjusted his rope. "I try to give her the benefit of the doubt, like if I can't see a brand from the distance, and all the other stuff is hers. I figger we probably miss a few of hers anyway, and Sully probably mavericked a few of Blair's along the way. I'd guess it comes out pretty even."

"Uh-huh." Quinn held back from saying anything more, but he was convinced that if anyone did much mavericking, it would have been Blair more than Sully. As things were shaping up with Newman's help, Sully was likely to be paying Mrs. Blair for some of Blair's cattle, some of his own, and some that didn't exist. Quinn shook his head and half-smiled. He thought he could understand Newman's generosity. Newman got along well with Mrs. Blair, and if he treated her well in these ways, he could compensate for the fur coat or any other favors he might have incurred.

On the third day, which Quinn expected to be their last day at this job, they had met to mark down numbers and were taking a breather. As usual, Quinn wrote down the numbers Newman gave him; by now he had decided he would give the numbers to Sully along with a comment that Newman's figures might be generous estimates in some places.

At the present, Quinn and Newman were stopped southwest of the Blair place, in a landscape of breaks and hills. They were sitting on the ground on a high spot and letting their horses rest. Quinn had put the tally book in his pocket, and Newman was smoking a cigarette. The midday sun was shining overhead, and for early November the weather was not bad.

Newman was looking off to the west, with a

thoughtful look on his face. "You know," he said, "if I thought the weather would hold out like this, and what with the little bit of extra wages I get from Sully, I might see about gettin' out of here after all."

Quinn motioned with his head. "Oregon?"

Newman nodded. "Same idea as before."

They sat for a few more minutes without speaking, and Newman pinched out his cigarette with his gloved thumb and forefinger. He stood up and put the toe of his boot on it, and as he was moving his boot back and forth he suddenly stopped.

"See something?" Quinn asked.

Newman crouched back down next to Quinn and pointed to the west. "Off over there. I saw somethin' move in that header."

Quinn looked at the draw Newman was pointing at. "Animal?"

Newman shook his head. "Looked different. I think it was someone on a horse." He turned and looked at Quinn. "Could be someone out here tryin' to make off with Blair's stuff."

"Sully's, now."

"Uh-huh." Newman was looking intently at the landscape.

"Well, whoever it is, if he doesn't come up out of there, it's hard for us to see him or for him to see us."

Newman spit on the ground in front of where he crouched, forearms on his knees. "I think if he doesn't show his head in another five minutes, we could slip on down there and see about gettin' a closer look."

"I'll count to three hundred," Quinn said. He counted to himself as the two of them sat in silence. When he reached the end he gave it a few more seconds and then said, "That's it."

The two men rose to their feet. Newman took off his right glove and reached into his blanket-lined coat. He drew out a pistol, which was a little smaller than the .45 six-shooters that both Quinn and Newman carried in their saddlebags. The pistol looked like a double-action Lightning model, and this was the first time Quinn had seen it. He figured it was Newman's hideout gun, and he supposed it always rode in Newman's coat. Quinn recalled Newman's habit of patting the tan coat when it was tied to the back of the saddle.

Quinn watched as Newman clicked the cylinder all the way around. A man liked to keep track of the next man's firearms as well as his own, so Quinn watched as Newman stopped the cylinder on an empty chamber and let the hammer down on it. Newman gave Quinn a half-comical wink as he put the gun away and put his glove back on his hand. Then the two men mounted up and rode down and across the upper end of the breaks.

As they rode past each draw to their left, they looked down into it, just as if they were checking for cattle. This country had been grazed pretty close and had few cattle in it at the present, so there wasn't much to catch the eye.

When they came to the last draw they decided to ride down into the bottom, which looked like a broad drainage sloping away to the south. The going was smooth and they picked up the pace, coming out of the bottom at a quick trot.

About a half-mile ahead, two riders were heading south. The horses were walking, swishing their tails. Both horses were dark, with no flashes of white socks or pinto splotches.

"Wonder if we might catch up with them jaspers," Newman said. "Ask 'em if they've seen any TJ cattle."

"Sounds all right," said Quinn, nudging his horse into a lope.

Before long, one of the distant riders turned around and looked back. Then the two dark horses broke into a run and moved away. Dust rose in their wake, and the distance between the two pairs of riders began to lengthen. The two dark horses carried their riders up and over a rise, and then they dropped from sight.

Newman and Quinn slowed their horses back down to a walk.

"That's probably about as much as we're gonna know," said Quinn. "They've been out nosin' around here, and they don't want us to get a closer look."

"Vultures," said Newman. "Seein' what they can pick up after a dead man."

"Could be," Quinn commented. Then to himself he admitted that it could be something else. It could be the avenger Larkin, who could have picked up a helper by now. Word had probably gotten around Hartville that Sully had bought out Blair's holdings and had a couple of men out taking a count.

Quinn and Newman finished their tally that day, and the next morning they headed back to the Lockhart headquarters. They left all of Blair's horses at Spring Creek and rode the two Lockhart horses they had each started with. Additionally, Quinn brought back his own packhorse, which Newman had taken with him on the return from the mountains.

Quinn had the comfortable feeling that he was going to have everything in one place again, and he supposed Newman might feel the same. Newman had packed all his own gear, including the raccoon coat, and apparently had settled with Mrs. Blair. He had not kept Quinn waiting for long outside with the horses, and he came out of the house light-footed and whistling.

At the Lockhart Ranch they dropped their gear at the bunkhouse and took their horses into the barn. Newman said he would take care of the horses while Quinn gave his report to the boss.

Sully was standing on the porch, so Quinn walked up the steps and showed him the tally book. Quinn flipped the pages and explained the notations, and as he handed the book to Sully he said, "Newman's count might be a little generous in some places, but it's probably not far off. At any rate, I don't think we'll come out long." Then, as an afterthought, he told Sully about the two riders he and Newman had seen.

Sully's eyes closed and he gave two quick nods. Then his eyes opened and he said, "Good enough, Quinn. I'll talk to you in a little while."

At noon dinner, Sully came into the bunkhouse as usual and put his hat on a peg. When he was finished eating he said he wanted Sipe and Newman to ride down to Blair's and bring back the horses. He told them to look over the mounts, trim up any bad feet, and then turn the string in with the main herd. Then he said he wanted Dexter and Quinn to take the wagon down to Blair's and to take Mrs. Blair into Hartville. He said that he had told her he would help her that far and that she knew where she wanted to go from there.

Quinn and Dexter had driven about half the way to Blair's when they met Sipe and Newman coming back with the horses in a cloud of dust. The two men on horseback had gotten a head start to begin with, and they were moving fast, which was the best way to herd horses. Newman, loping in the lead, waved to the men in the wagon. The nine bareback horses were strung out behind him, running loose but all following, and Sipe took up the rear.

He swung in beside the wagon for a moment. He took off the dark hat with the troughed brim, wiped the cuff of his jacket sleeve across his forehead, and smiled. "She's expectin' you," he said. "I imagine she'll still have some pie left when you git there." Quinn and Dexter thanked him, and he turned and rode off after the horses.

Mrs. Blair did indeed have some pie waiting for them—an apricot pie, made of dried apricots, with a pot of coffee to go along with it. She told the men not to hurry, but she also said she would prefer to go into Hartville that evening if they didn't mind. Quinn and Dexter said it would be fine.

When they had finished their pie and coffee, she showed them the baggage she had stacked in the front room. It consisted of two wooden trunks, a gladstone bag, a leather valise, and a carpet traveling bag. Quinn asked if that was all, and she said, yes, everything else would stay except for some blankets she would use on the way into town.

Quinn and Dexter loaded the trunks and bags while she washed the dishes and put the kitchen in order. Darkness was beginning to gather inside the house as Quinn and Dexter stood in the kitchen and Mrs. Blair went through the rooms. Then she came back out to the kitchen with two wool blankets in her arms.

"I'm ready," she said.

Quinn opened the door and she walked out, not looking back. Dexter went out next. Quinn took a last look around before shutting the door. The kitchen was clean and bare, and the deer antlers hung stark above the sideboard in the dusk.

Mrs. Blair said she preferred to ride in the box, so she nestled down among her bags and covered herself with the blankets. Quinn and Dexter sat on the wagon seat, with a large robe and canvas sheet draped over their laps.

The sun went down and the world darkened. Then the moon rose in the east, a half moon that shed some light on the trail ahead. Except for the clip-clop of the horses and the creak of the wagon, Quinn heard no other sounds. The moon rose higher and a little breeze came up, wafting the smell of cedar as the trail wound through a pass in the hills north of Hartville.

Not long after that they pulled into town, where lights and noises poured out in small quantities from the buildings, and feet sounded on board sidewalks while here and there a voice carried on the cold night air. What few people were out—all men—were going from one place to another and not lounging on the street.

Mrs. Blair said she would like to be left off at a boardinghouse where she had stayed when she had first come to Wyoming the year before. Dexter knew where it was, so in a very little while they had Mrs. Blair and her belongings safely indoors.

She thanked the men and tried to give them a five-dollar gold piece, but they would not take it.

"God bless you," she said, and for the first time Quinn saw her eyes moisten with tears.

"Good luck, ma'am," Dexter said, taking off his hat with the worn crown.

Quinn took off his hat also and added, "The best of luck to you, Mrs. Blair."

Then they were back in the wagon with their

hats on, turning in the middle of the street. Dexter, who was driving, turned to Quinn and said in a low voice, "I don't care for this town. I'd just as soon pull out."

"Fine with me," said Quinn. He looked around and saw no one within hearing distance, so he leaned toward Dexter and added, "I'd rather sleep out under the stars than in this place. The less time we spend here, the better."

They were going back through the main part of town now, where the lights from inside the buildings cast a dull glow into the street. Muffled sounds came from within, and occasionally a door opened to let clearer sounds into the night air.

Quinn looked ahead and saw two horsemen coming toward the wagon. One of the riders turned off into a dark side street, and the two men spoke to each other as they parted. Although Quinn could not hear the words, he gathered from the tone of voice that they were saying good-night or see-you-later.

The remaining horse and rider, a dark form in the dull light, continued down the street in the direction of the wagon. Quinn watched the form without thinking, and then, at a distance of about forty yards, he felt a twinge of recognition. It was the flat-crowned hat—and the slouch. The rider came nearer, and without looking directly at him, Quinn took in the dark wool overcoat and dark gloves, then a dark muffler covering the lower part of the face. Quinn knew that in better light he would have been able to see light brown eyes in a yellow background; but even in the poor light he could see gray in the dark hair, and a scowl on the upper half of the face. Then, as the rider passed, Quinn saw the detail that left no doubt. The dull light in the street gave a faint shine to the rattlesnake hatband.

Chapter Thirteen

Quinn watched his frosty breath rise in the moon-lit night as he lay on his back. Dexter was asleep already, and it was probably close to midnight. They had driven out of Hartville and had headed straight for the ranch, which caused them to bypass Blair's place by a couple of miles. At some distance north of Blair's they had stopped, set the horses out to graze, and rolled out their beds. The ground was cold, but not as cold as a wagon box with cold air circulating beneath it, so they set their beds side by side on the ground with the wagon robe and canvas draped over both of them.

It was a clear night, cold but not unbearable. The chilly air was invigorating to someone who couldn't sleep, and Quinn lay thinking as he gazed at the stars above. Now that he had delivered Mrs. Blair, he supposed his obligations with Sully were over for the season. He would be free to visit Marie, to help her with a few jobs around her place if she liked. He could stay on at the Lockhart and do his visiting from there—maybe help Moose wrangle firewood to earn some of his keep.

He heard one of the horses stamp where it was picketed and grazing, and then he heard it snort. He closed his eyes and heard the horse snuffle again.

Something in the sound brought back the image of Larkin, the dark avenger riding in the cold night. Quinn wondered who the other man was who had just taken leave of Larkin, and he wondered if the two of them might be the two jaspers he and Newman had seen out on the range. If Larkin had picked up a helper in Hartville, Quinn could imagine who it might be. Cater would be the type to nourish a pointless grudge and then, when he couldn't do anything about it himself, to throw in with someone else who might.

He couldn't be sure it was Cater, though. For one thing, there was a mismatch with the horses, as Cater had always ridden a gray horse before. Still, he could have been riding a dark horse that day, for all that. Or Larkin could have picked up someone else, or the two jaspers could have been two other men entirely.

Quinn let out a sigh and turned onto his side. Better to think about girls, he thought. Pretty girls, with long dark hair and swishing dresses and the smell of lilacs and the soft pressure of a hand resting on his forearm.

He heard Dexter's early-morning cough and remembered where he was. It was gray morning, he had frost in his mustache, and his feet were cold.

" 'Bout time to get up?" he asked, with his back to his sleeping partner.

Dexter's voice came back from the other side. "Prob'ly so. Wouldn't it be nice to have some of that pie and coffee now?"

"I think the first coffee we're gonna get today is back at the Lockhart," Quinn answered. He reached for his hat and put it on as he rolled out of bed. He lifted his coat, which had been his pillow, and put it on as well. Then he shook out his boots, put them on, and stood up to settle into them. He shivered as he made water on a clump of sagebrush, and then the shivering went away. Moving around would help him warm up. He fetched the horses, brought them to the back of the wagon, and fed them each a nosebag of oats.

Dexter had turned out by now, and the two of them rolled up their beds and the top covers. After a few more minutes the horses were through eating, so the men hitched up and set out on their way again. It was a cold, clear morning, and the details of the landscape stood out sharply as Quinn drove the wagon north.

When the sun was up but not very high, the trail led down through a draw and up onto a rise. A quarter mile ahead and off to the left a little, Quinn saw a mule deer buck. The animal had a full set of antlers, which caught the glint of the morning sun. Quinn looked at Dexter and motioned with his head toward the deer.

"Let's see how close we can get," Dexter said.

Quinn gave a nod and drove on.

The deer watched them until they were within about eighty yards, and then he turned and bounced away to the east, his antlers flashing as they moved up and down in the sunlight.

Dexter gave a low, little laugh. "I wouldn't have minded havin' a rifle right then. He'd 've made good steaks."

"I bet."

"Uh-huh. Nothin' like nice deer steaks off a fat buck like that one, sizzled in some of Moose's bacon grease."

Quinn could feel his stomach growling. "First it was pie and coffee, and now it's venison steak. That kind of talk makes me hungrier."

"We could talk about something else."

"Like what?"

Dexter grinned. "What else is there?"

Quinn nodded and smiled back. "Yeh, but

talkin' about them doesn't do any good, either."

Newman had his dun horse saddled and was tying on his gear when Quinn and Dexter pulled into the ranch. Newman had wrapped the fur coat in a piece of canvas, with fur sticking out of both ends, and was tying it onto the front of his saddle. It looked like a wolf or coyote draped over the swells.

Quinn and Dexter waved, then pulled up by the cottonwood tree. Dexter said he would take care of the horses, and Quinn understood Dexter was giving him a few minutes to say good-bye to his working partner.

Newman was coming out of the bunkhouse with his warbag and bedroll when Quinn walked across the yard.

"Headin' on out?"

Newman settled the bedroll behind the saddle. " 'Bout time, I guess." He had his back to Quinn and did not turn to look at him.

"Uh-huh."

"Weather's still holdin' out." Newman tied the saddle strings to hold down the bedroll.

Quinn measured his words. "A fella wants to be careful."

Newman seemed to pause with his canvas bag in midair; then he set it on top of the bedroll and tied it on. He glanced at Quinn and said, "Always."

"Just a word of warning." Quinn spoke in a

lower voice—not so low as to sound secretive and attract attention, but low enough not to broadcast what he had to say.

Newman turned, half facing Quinn, with his forearm leaning against the saddle. He tipped his head up and said, "Yeh?"

"You remember I mentioned runnin' into a fellow down in Chugwater, name of Larkin?"

Newman squinted his left eye against the sun and nodded.

"And he was lookin' for a man named Slade."

Newman's head barely moved, but it made an affirmative motion. Then he said, "What does that have to do with me?"

For the moment, Quinn could see only the top of Newman's hat. "I don't know," he said. "Maybe nothing. But if it means something, I thought I should tell you I saw him last night in Hartville."

"Who?"

"Larkin."

Newman leaned forward and let a gob of saliva drop to the ground. Then he looked Quinn in the eyes and shook his head. "I don't know anyone named Larkin."

Quinn knew he had to pick his words carefully. Newman was still his friend, and it wouldn't do to ask a prying question. "Well," he said, "it's just somethin' I caught wind of, and I thought it might mean somethin' if you knew of anyone named Slade or Corbeau."

Quinn thought he saw Newman tense up, but

if he did it was only for a second. "I don't believe you've mentioned that last name before."

"Maybe not. But the way the story goes, Larkin is out to settle a score on behalf of a man named Corbeau."

Newman looked straight at Quinn again. The blue eyes were cool as the November sky. "You were right, Quinn." He paused for a second, still looking steady. "When you said a man has got to be careful."

Quinn's face tightened. "Meanin' me?"

Newman's eyebrows went up. "Meanin' you, or me, or this other fella, or anyone else. But you were right."

Quinn took a deep breath and gave it another try. "For all I know, he could have been one of those two riders we saw down south the other day."

"Might could be." Newman's tone was dead neutral.

"Just before I saw him last night, he split up with another man. I didn't get a good look at the other one, but it made me think there might be two of 'em, and they might be the same two."

Newman shrugged, as if it was none of his worry.

"Just thought I'd mention it, in case any of it meant anything."

Newman's face relaxed into a half-smile. "Damn little of it does, Quinn. Damn little."

Quinn forced a smile. "So are you headin' out right away?"

"Yep." Newman turned and checked his cinch.

"Goin' west?"

"Uh-huh. Through Devil's Gate and on out that-a-way." Newman untied the horse.

"Well, I'll wish you good luck." Quinn put out his hand.

Newman shook his hand and looked him in the eyes. "Good luck to you, too, Quinn. It's been good to know you."

"Same here."

"Well, I'll say good-bye to Dexter and be on my way. I've already said the rest of my good-byes." Newman walked his horse over to the barn.

Quinn went to the wagon where it stood unhitched by the bare cottonwood tree. He reached in for the bedrolls, and when he looked around he saw Newman swing his leg up and over the back of the saddle.

"So long, Quinn," he called out as he rode away.

"So long, Newman. Good luck." Quinn watched the tan coat and dun horse move away until the two colors disappeared behind a rise in the ground.

Quinn lay on his bunk for a midmorning rest, his hands folded behind his head. He felt as if Newman had given him the brush-off. After all the time they had spent working together, he would have expected a little more confidence at the end. He was sure Newman was Slade—a man who had run out on his partner and didn't want to talk about it. Newman was out for himself, and that was it. He had been that way with Blair, too—and Mrs. Blair, from the looks of it.

For all the times they had worked and talked and joked together, Newman had been noncommittal. Maybe he had to be that way to keep the doors closed on his past, but to Quinn it seemed as if the self-protection ran in a deeper grain. It was Newman's nature, he thought, to isolate himself. He remembered Newman hunched inside the coonskin coat, insulated from the world.

Quinn felt a bitter smile come to his face. Newman was really more like a coyote, with a sly grin on his chops as he looked back over his shoulder. The Indians liked the coyote, thought he was a clever fellow. The white men, especially ranchers, hated him for killing calves and lambs. But the coyote himself probably had no sense of being good or bad, kind or cruel. He just was. If something was good or bad, it was in terms of his own survival. A weak lamb was good; the shiny, dark thing a man pointed at him was bad.

That was the way Newman was. If he had run out on his partner, he probably did not see it as bad but as something he had to do. If he lived his whole life on the run, he probably saw it as just a necessary way of life.

Quinn thought of Larkin, the dark rider in pursuit. The man was no doubt sure he was in the

Dexter looked at Quinn. "How about you?"

"I don't know."

"Aw, come on. The more of us there are, the better we can put the squeeze on him."

"All right," Quinn said. "But I'll let one of you fellows shoot him."

The next morning, the three of them set out in the dark. Dexter and Quinn agreed on the place where they had seen the buck, and when the three men were within half a mile of the spot, they fanned out.

Quinn rode on the east, thinking he might drive the deer toward the other two men, who both carried rifles. The sun came up in a pale sky, slowly washing the rangeland from gray to yellow to tan. Quinn rode slowly, scanning the landscape as he circled to the east and then back to the west. He expected every moment to hear the boom of a rifle shot, but the time dragged on in silence.

The sun was at his back now, casting a short shadow in front of him and the horse. About half a mile away, where he expected the trail to be, he saw two riders headed north. It would not be Sipe and Dexter, he thought. They would still be spread out, and they would be headed south if they were moving at all.

The two riders dipped out of sight, so Quinn took the opportunity to find a low spot for himself and his horse.

He let a long time pass without seeing or hearing anything. He did not want to meet the other riders, and he wanted to let Sipe and Dexter hunt the deer anyway. The sun felt warm on his back as he stood by the horse, but his feet got cold. He looked at the sun and decided that if he walked to get his feet warmed up, he would get back to the meeting place at about the right time. Leading the horse, he set off on foot.

Still he heard nothing except the sound of his boots and the horse's hooves. He felt warmer now, and relaxed, although he still expected the crash of a rifle at any moment. He walked on, across the broad, quiet country.

He found Sipe and Dexter kneeling with their backs to a low gray bluff and facing the sun. They were holding their horses' reins, but the horses stood off to each side and did not block the sunlight. Both men were smoking, so Quinn assumed they were finished hunting.

When Quinn had come within thirty yards, Dexter spoke. "See anything?"

"No deer. Just a couple of riders. How about you?"

"The same. Sipe saw them fellers, too. I didn't."

Sipe put his palm over his pipe and puffed out a cloud of smoke. "Looked like our old friend Cater and someone else."

"Is that right? Did the other one have a dark coat and hat, with a flat crown?"

Sipe looked up. "Yeh. You know him?"

"I think it's that fellow Larkin." Quinn looked at

Dexter. "He passed us on the street there in Hartville."

Dexter held his cigarette down in front of him and looked up at Quinn. "I didn't notice."

"Just as we were leaving town. After we left off the missus."

"Oh." Dexter looked at Sipe and then back at Quinn. "What do you think they're doin' out here?"

Quinn ran his tongue across his lips. "Hunting a man named Slade, I'd bet."

Dexter and Sipe exchanged a glance, and then Dexter asked Quinn, "Any idea who that might be?"

"Probably the same idea you've got."

Dexter took another pull on his cigarette and then dropped the butt on the ground, where he crushed it with his boot. "Newman has a pretty good lead on 'em." He looked again at Quinn. "He said he was going out by Devil's Gate, didn't he?"

Quinn nodded. "That's what he said."

Sipe took the pipe out of his mouth. "I imagine they'll ask around about him, or already have. I doubt they want to jump him right on the ranch."

Dexter pulled a stem of grass and put it in his mouth. "He might not be that easy to find."

Sipe was smiling. "Sooner or later, somewhere along the line," he said, "I'd bet he meets up with his little Mohee."

Dexter gave him a sidelong glance. "Not to mention any names."

"He called her Lou Ellen when we was eatin' pie."

Quinn lay in his bed in the dark. The bunkhouse was quiet except for the light snores and even breathing of the other men. Quinn couldn't drop off to sleep, though, because he was haunted by the image of a tan figure pursued by a dark one. Then there was Cater for good measure. For as much as Quinn had felt perturbed at Newman for holding out on him, he couldn't get over the idea that there were two men who wanted to hunt down a man who had been his friend.

It came back to that. Despite everything, Newman had been his friend. The man had helped get him a job to begin with, and he had never done anything outright to cause Quinn to distrust him. Newman had been evasive about his own past, but he had not pried into Quinn's. In day-to-day things he had sided with Quinn the way a fellow cowhand should, like the time he helped him with the bucking horse.

Newman was Slade, he was sure now more than ever. But even at that, he couldn't make assumptions about the degree of the man's guilt. After all, he hadn't run out on Blair. If he had skipped out on Corbeau, he might have had his reasons. And if it really mattered, Quinn could ask him more directly—if he ever saw him again. Maybe Newman didn't have a conscience, but he was still a friend.

On one hand, Quinn told himself Newman

could ride his own trail, come what may. On the other, he knew there were two men following that trail, and if he, Quinn, sat by idly when he could have done something about it, he could have reason to feel guilty later.

Chapter Fourteen

Quinn swung his rope three times and dropped the loop over the head of his saddle horse. The brown horse was used to being caught, and although he hadn't been ridden very much lately he followed Quinn without any trouble.

Quinn talked to the horse as he brushed it down and combed out its mane and tail. He put on the pad and blanket and saddle, cinched his rig, and slipped on the bridle. He coiled up the lead rope and tucked it along with the halter into the saddlebag closest to him, where he also carried a picket pin. Then he led the horse to the hitching rail in front of the bunkhouse.

He would have preferred to fit out his packhorse, but he knew he would travel faster with one horse, and the man he hoped to catch up with was traveling with only one horse also. A cold wind was starting to blow from the northwest, and the chill reminded him to pack carefully.

He folded his blankets the long way and rolled them in their canvas sheet, then tied the bedroll across the swells of his saddle to cut the wind. He was already wearing a wool overcoat, a thick wool shirt, heavy wool pants, long underwear, and double socks, and he had stuffed his warbag with more socks, heavy mittens, a knitted wool cap, and an extra shirt. Also in the bag he had packed jerky, raisins, dried apples, and two cans of tomatoes. The bag seemed heavy when he hefted it, but he could easily imagine needing everything that was in it.

With his rope on the left side as usual, he tied a full canteen on the right side. In his empty saddlebag he put an extra pair of gloves, two dozen hardtack biscuits, and a small cloth bag of coffee. He did not know if he would have a chance even to make coffee, but it was the lightest item in his pack. The horse was weighted down pretty well, he thought, and it might take him a few days to accomplish what he was setting out to do, but he had made up his mind.

The other three men in the bunkhouse had expressed no opinion, but Quinn could tell they thought he was wasting his effort. They had liked Newman well enough, he supposed, but they had been friends among themselves for a couple of seasons, and they had formed no special bond with Newman. He rode for the brand, but when it came down to it, he was just another smiling chuck line rider. Quinn could tell that was how the others saw Newman; it was in their jokes when he was here, and it was in their jokes when he was gone.

Quinn put his left foot in the stirrup and swung his right leg high and wide over the bag he had tied to the back of the saddle. He adjusted his reins, pulled his hat on snug, and rode out of the yard of the Lockhart Ranch.

It was a gray morning without direct sunlight, as a high cloud cover filled the sky from east to west. The wind cut at him crossways as he rode out of the shelter of the ranch headquarters.

He knew he was behind to start with. Newman had almost a two-day lead on him, while Larkin was a full day behind that. Quinn felt he had an advantage in being more familiar with cold country, but he had no assurance he could catch up soon. Of the other two parties, he thought Newman would go the fastest, as he was in the lead and didn't have to read someone else's trail. However, he liked the campfire and his warm bedding, and Quinn didn't know how much of a sense of urgency the man felt. If he didn't hear the bloodhounds on his trail, he might dawdle awhile here and there. Larkin would travel slower, especially if he separated and rejoined with Cater as they asked questions and followed dead ends along Newman's trail. Larkin, too, was from warmer country, which could slow him down as well.

Even if he was as far behind as he was, Quinn knew he had to stop at Marie's. It was almost on the way, he told himself, and he wouldn't stay long.

He caught the smell of wood smoke from a quarter mile out, as the wind was blowing in his direction. The sun had still not broken through the high clouds, so the weathered house looked bleak in the cold morning.

As he rode into the yard he called a greeting. A horse answered from the stable, and as he shifted his gaze from the kitchen door to the stable, he saw movement. The stable door opened, and Marie stepped out. She was wearing a winter cap with ear lugs and below that a dark gray wool ulster, or overcoat, which reached almost to her ankles. He felt a spark inside, and he raised a hand to answer her wave.

"You look like you're going somewhere," she said after he had dismounted and stepped clear from his horse. Her face looked bright and pretty, framed by her dark hair on both sides, the short-billed cap, and the closed neck of the overcoat.

"I am," he said. He watched her eyes travel over the items tied down on the horse. "But I expect to be back."

Her eyes returned to meet his. "Do I dare ask what's taking you out in this weather?"

"I need to go warn a friend," he said. "He's got a couple of fellows after him."

Her face froze in its frame. "Where is he?"

"He's already gone, and they're behind him. It's my friend Newman, that I worked with all summer and fall."

Her face picked up a little bit of expression as she gave him a questioning look.

"He was already leaving, and he might have known—I'll say he did know—that one of these men was lookin' for him. But it looks more serious than I think he realizes, and I want to get to him." He could tell his words sounded too sketchy, even to his own ears as he said them, so he gave her the background of Larkin, Corbeau, and Slade.

She listened without interrupting, and when he was done she said, "I can tell you've made up your mind to go, and I wouldn't try to talk you out of it, but I wonder why you would want to get in the middle of it."

He had asked himself the same question, but he hadn't tried to put the whole answer into words until now. "Part of it is, I guess he deserves it. We rode together, and I wouldn't be able to forgive myself if I found out they got to him and I knew I could have done something." He hesitated. "And the other part is, I guess I just need to ask him if he ran out on his partner the way they said he did."

Her eyes seemed to be roving over his face. "I suppose there was no way to ask him that already?"

He shook his head. "No, but it was probably my fault. I could have pushed it. But now I feel I've got to ask, especially if I'm going to all this trouble."

Marie had a faint smile on her face. "Because he's your friend, you'll risk your own safety, and then you hope to find out if he's the kind of friend that's worth it."

Quinn laughed, a short and nervous laugh. "That's about it." He paused. "But I felt I needed to come by and tell you." He touched his chest. "And somewhere in here, I figured you'd understand."

He lowered his gloved left hand and moved it toward her. Her right hand, also gloved, moved to touch it.

"I'm glad you came by," she said. "And I hope you come back." Her dark eyes looked soft, as if they were going to moisten, but they didn't. "Be careful, Quinn."

He tried to give her a smile of assurance. "I will." He stood for a long second in the chilly gray morning, his reins in his right hand and a woman's hand in his left. He knew that if he didn't say it now, he would be unhappy with himself when he rode away. So he blurted out, "There's somethin' I want to tell you."

He felt an uneasy pressure in her hand, as if it began to move away from him and then relented.

"What is it?" she asked.

"The first time I saw you," he began, "before

we even met, we had a little rainstorm out this way."

"I remember that. I was taking in the clothes."

"Well, shortly after I saw you, that's when it rained. A nice, pretty rain. And after that I saw a rainbow. A double rainbow."

Her face relaxed into a smile. "A rainbow is supposed to be good luck."

He smiled in return. "For me it was. Because then I got to meet you." Her hand felt relaxed in his, so he went on. "What I'm wondering now is whether a double rainbow means double good look or good luck for two people."

"It might be either," she said.

"I don't know, but I think you have to believe in good luck to begin with."

"Do you?"

He nodded. "And you?"

She gave a closemouthed smile and then said, "Yes."

They moved toward each other, and he thought he could feel her hand waver as he himself was trembling. Their lips met and came apart, and then Quinn was looking into her eyes, a little closer than before but with their joined hands between them.

"Be careful," she said. "And good luck."

"Thank you, Marie. Good luck to you, too." Then he mounted the brown horse and rode away.

When he was out on the trail and had settled into his ride, he remembered how he had seen her, bulky in the long drab overcoat. He thought he must have looked different to her, too, bundled in thick clothing as he was. But beneath it, he knew they were the same two people as before, getting to know each other.

He recalled the instant he had seen her stepping out of the stable door. He had seen a form and recognized it. It reminded him of the way horses recognized people. From a quarter of a mile across a pasture, one of his horses would know him, whether he was wearing thick clothing or thin, a hat or a cap. He had recognized her before he realized it, and something inside him had responded. Remembering her now, he thought she had been as pretty as he had ever seen her.

He rode west, planning to catch the trail he assumed Newman had followed. The road followed the Platte as it curved north and west around the Laramie Mountains. Quinn did not know the trail beyond Casper, but he knew it angled southwest from there, passing Independence Rock and Devil's Gate as it moved into the Sweetwater country. Somewhere out there, he might catch up.

He crossed the river south of Orin and followed the trail north. All the trees were long out of leaf now, and the landscape looked stark in its dull colors. The day was moving into midafternoon without the sun having broken through, and even a sunny day at this time of the year would be short. Quinn thought he might ride on into the night for a ways if he had any moonlight at all.

An object appeared on the trail ahead, and Quinn felt a jolt in his stomach. It was a dark object, standing out against the pale background in the dull light of the afternoon. It stayed on the trail, gradually becoming larger as Quinn approached. He had known from the first instant that it was not an animal by itself—not a cow or a horse or even a buffalo. Now he saw for sure that it was a man on a horse, apparently waiting for him.

Closer now, he saw clearer details in the outline of the rider—a dark coat, a flat-crowned hat, a slouched posture.

Quinn stopped his horse within a few yards of the other man and horse. They were not blocking the trail but were off to the left side, facing it at a forty-five-degree angle. The other man must have set himself that way to have his back hunched against the wind.

"Good afternoon," said Quinn.

"Good afternoon. Headin' north?" The man was giving him a good looking-over.

Quinn tipped his head in a nod.

The man's yellow teeth showed as he spoke. "Cold wetheh."

"That it is. And it's bound to get colder." As Quinn spoke, he took a quick glance at the man. He saw again the dark, graying hair, the yellowed eyes, the stubbled face. The man had a muffler draped around his neck and hanging in front; Quinn supposed he had unwrapped it from his face in order to meet the oncoming rider.

Quinn looked at the man's hands. They were gloved and both resting on the saddle horn, Quinn's glance flickered to his own hands, also in plain view on his saddle horn, above the draped bedroll. There was no need to make a stranger nervous by leaving one hand out of sight. Quinn knew his own gun was covered by his coat, but he knew Larkin would assume he carried one, just as he assumed there was a gun and holster beneath the man's heavy overcoat. Quinn also supposed Larkin carried a rifle, although it was not in sight on the right side of his horse.

"Too damn cold." The man's voice had a bitter tone.

"Headin' south?" Quinn asked, enjoying his own show of innocence.

"Not yit. But I don' aim to spend all winter here."

"Uh-huh."

The man pointed his chin at Quinn's outfit. "How far north you goin'?"

Quinn thought fast. This man would talk to Cater sooner or later. "Just across the river tonight," he said. "If I can't get a winter job over in Shawnee, workin' in a coal mine, I might go on up to the Powder River country. I've got friends there."

The other man wiped his right hand across the bottom of his nose. "You a coal miner?"

Quinn knew the man had noticed his rope and spurs. "Not when there's cows to punch. But most of the ranch work's over for right now."

The yellow teeth showed, and Quinn thought he heard the man say, "That's a bet."

Quinn said, "Uh-huh," and shifted his hands on the pommel.

"Well, don't let me keep you," the other man said. "You've got a ways to go, and so have I."

Quinn touched his right hand to his hat brim and said, "Good enough. Pleased to meet you."

The dark hat tipped, showing the hatband, and the voice said, "Same here."

Quinn was relaxing into the single motion of moving his reins forward and putting his heels to the horse when the voice came back.

"Do I know you?"

Quinn and the horse stopped. Quinn met the man's eyes, filmy brown eyes in a yellow background. It seemed to Quinn as if the man had pulled himself together and was trying to stare him down. Quinn gave him a steady look back and said, "I don't think so." He let the silence hang for a couple of seconds and then said, "My name's Quinn."

"Mine's Lawkin."

"Larkin?"

"Thet's it."

"Well, pleased to meet you," Quinn said again.

"The same here." Larkin relaxed into his slouch and looked back dawn the trail behind Quinn. He tossed the tail of his muffler over his left shoulder, covering the lower half of his face.

"Have a good trip," said Quinn, now moving his horse forward.

"The same to you," came the voice.

Quinn rode forward and did not look back for a couple of hundred yards. When he did turn and look back, he saw a rider coming up out of the trees in the river bottom and riding toward Larkin.

The rider was not hard to recognize. He was a husky man on a big gray horse. He wore a round-brimmed hat with a peaked crown, and beneath the hat the pale hair and mustache caught the afternoon light.

Quinn thought back quickly and realized he hadn't looked at the trail to count tracks as he had been riding up to meet Larkin. He hadn't noticed if someone had pulled off the trail to go down into the trees. Cater might have been behind him all the time he was stopped to talk, or the man might have gone down into the trees for natural reasons and was just now coming out.

Whatever the case, Quinn knew one thing. For the time being at least, he was out on the trail ahead of the other two. That was bad, because he had them at his back, but it was good if he could get out ahead even farther.

He crossed the river again, because they expected him to. The brown horse had held up well, and Quinn decided to ride on for another hour or so until full darkness set in. He followed the river almost due west now, and when he thought the horse had done enough for the day, he made a cold camp. He followed a dry wash about two hundred yards back from the river, unloaded the horse, and picketed it in a grassy area.

That night he ate four dry biscuits and a can of cold tomatoes. He walked all the way to the river and rinsed out the can, thinking he could use it to boil coffee if he had a fire in some later camp.

Feeble moonlight came through the high clouds as Quinn settled into his blankets. The wind had died down at dusk, and he could hear the horse clearly as it shifted its feet and grazed. He had taken off his hat, coat, and boots and had put on a wool cap. Snuggled in his bedroll with the coat for a pillow, he began to feel the warmth gather.

He thought of Sipe and Dexter, back at the warm bunkhouse. He wondered if they would go out and hunt the big deer again. They hadn't seemed very disappointed at not finding it the first time, but they spoke well of deer meat.

Quinn remembered the butchered deer that Newman had told him to toss aside. He supposed it was pretty well eaten by now, what with the ground critters and the birds. It had been a good chunk of meat. Then he thought again of the big buck, and he imagined the thick, dark steaks that would come off the haunch of a deer like that. As he lay in the dark, remembering the cold biscuits and tomatoes he had eaten for supper, he thought of rich deer steaks, sputtering in a pool of bacon grease in one of Moose's cast-iron skillets.

He awoke to a cold, gray morning. The wind had not yet picked up, and the horse was still grazing at the end of its tether. Quinn rolled out of bed, pulled on his hat and coat and boots, put on his gloves, and took the horse to water. Back at camp he set the horse to graze again while he rolled up his gear.

The wind came up then, and with it a few light snowflakes. Quinn lost no time getting the horse saddled and packed; then he stood with the horse blocking the wind as he ate cold biscuits and raisins for his breakfast.

As he ate, he watched the trail below, where it crossed the opening of the draw as it ran along the river. The snow was still light, so he could see the trail and the trees of the river bottom beyond. It was the type of scene in which a person could expect to see a deer, but instead, a pair of horses came into view. Quinn felt his insides sink as he recognized the riders.

Larkin and Cater were riding hunched into the wind, their horses moving at a fast walk. The hoofbeats on dry ground were faintly audible, and no other sound carried. Neither of the riders looked up the draw in Quinn's direction, so he stood as still as he could until the party moved out of sight.

In that first moment, Quinn felt a letdown at having lost what little advantage he had gained.

Then he told himself to take it easy and think things through. He led the horse closer to the river and found a screen of box elder trees that blocked out most of the wind and snow. He needed to let the other two get well ahead of him now, so he relaxed and tried to think of how to make the best of things as they now stood.

One advantage was that he no longer had the other two men at his back. It was better to have them pass him unawares than to have them come up on him from behind. If the snow continued to fall, it would make it harder for them to track Newman until they got closer to him. In the meanwhile, Quinn could let them do the tracking and question-asking, and he could follow them in the new snow. Then, if the snow came down heavier, he could reconsider his plan.

He thought a two-hour lead would be all right, so he stuck it out where he was. The storm did not get any stronger, and the snow melted for the first hour until it began to stick and pile up in the open areas around him. The horse found a little grass to crop but did not seem ravenous. So Quinn waited, imagining the two riders moving farther ahead. From time to time he got up and walked around to keep warm, then went back to stand by the horse and brush snow off the gear. Finally he decided to mount up and move on.

No other riders had come along in the meanwhile, so the tracks, pressed into light snow and covered with more light snow, were easy to follow. The hoofprints led west along the north side of the river for about ten miles until one point where the two men had done quite a bit of riding around. Then the tracks led down through the river bottom and out on the other side.

Quinn wondered how the men might have determined that their quarry had crossed here, and then he decided they had read the sign before much snow had gathered. Time had elapsed since then. At any rate, the river was fordable here. Perhaps the first man had crossed at this point, and certainly the next two had. Quinn went across, lifting his stirrups with his boots and coming out dry on the other side.

He dismounted and walked his horse out to the edge of the trees. There he saw the hoofprints lead right out to the main trail and head west again.

Quinn followed the trail for at least another ten miles, and the mountains on his left came closer. In the late afternoon he saw smoke threading into the sky above some trees to the west. He had smelled the smoke a few minutes earlier, and now he saw it. He moved in to the edge of the trees, dismounted, and went ahead on foot. The wind was still blowing as it had done all day, but only a few snowflakes were falling, so he he could see for several hundred yards ahead. A line of trees led down to the river, and he imagined he was coming to La Bonte Creek. He craned his neck and saw a clump of cabins up ahead, which would be the source of the wood smoke.

Quinn continued on foot, hugging the edge of the timber, until he came within a couple of hundred yards of the cabins. He tied his horse in a thicket of low trees and walked slowly back out to the trail. He followed it another seventy-five yards west until he came to a spot where the snow was trampled in a wide area. Apparently one man had waited while another had laid down a set of tracks to the cabins and back. Then both tracks headed south toward the mountains.

Quinn went back to his horse and stood for a while, thinking. He could go to the cabins and ask around, but he would only make himself conspicuous and would learn nothing the other two men hadn't. They were at least coyote bright and they seemed onto something here, so he decided to follow their lead.

He let the afternoon wear on a while longer, hoping that Larkin and Cater would set him a course and get out far enough ahead so that he would not stumble onto them before night.

Daylight was fading now as he followed the tracks south through patches of trees and then open spaces. The trail veered slowly, to the southeast and then to the east. The two sets of tracks did not waver, so Quinn imagined they were on a steady course. It looked as if the trail was doubling back, along the base of the mountains.

Quinn smiled to himself in the dusk. That was

like Newman, to let it be known loud and clear that he was going out through Independence Rock and Devil's Gate, and then to double back after a good start. If he made it, he could go to Cheyenne and catch a train west. Quinn smiled broadly and almost laughed. Or he could be going to meet up with the little Mohee, as Sipe suggested. From there it would be anybody's guess.

Chapter Fifteen

Quinn woke to the wail of coyotes. It was still night, cold and dark. The wind had died down a little at nightfall, and now the clouds overhead had broken up to let in the light of the crescent moon.

He had an idea of where Newman was headed at least, and he could picture the options. Newman might go straight to Cheyenne, or he could angle off at one point over halfway there and head southwest, going through Sybille Canyon and on to Rock River, Medicine Bow, and points west. There was also the possibility that he might cut back east and follow the North Platte that way, but it seemed less likely. Newman might mislead someone about the trail he was going to take, but when he smoked a cigarette at his leisure and talked about where he would like to go, he looked off to the west. He seemed to be headed there, one way or the other.

Quinn thought he would know about the Platte Valley possibility by the next afternoon. If the trail still carried them south along the base of the mountains, then Newman was headed for Cheyenne or for the Sybille Canyon. If that was the case, Quinn would try to catch him before the trail forked in those two directions.

Quinn heard the coyotes again as he held the wool cap on his head and tried to nestle deeper into his bedding. This was his second cold camp in a row, and the best he could make of it was to try to get plenty of sleep.

Morning broke clear and cold, with frost on the bedding and other gear. Quinn got up and got dressed, then checked on the horse. It gave a low whicker as he approached, and a cloud of steam rose from its nostrils and open mouth. Quinn looked the horse over, patting its neck and shoulder and back. It looked like it was in good shape so far.

For the first two hours he followed tracks from the day before. Then the tracks veered off toward a cove of rocks and scrub trees. A hundred yards south, fresh tracks came out and resumed the trail. Quinn deduced that the two men ahead of him had camped nearby and were about two hours ahead of him.

At midmorning Quinn saw a pair of coyotes hunting, and not long after that he saw an eagle floating against the blue sky. Before the sun was straight up, however, clouds began to gather on the peaks to the west. It looked as if it was going to snow again, and Quinn expected it would come down heavier this time.

In midafternoon he crossed the little valley where he and Newman had followed the creek up into the mountains to fetch Blair's camp equipment. The tracks led straight across the valley, so Quinn did not loiter.

By dusk the tracks were still headed south. The trail he was following lay a few miles west of the main road, closer to the base of the mountains. It did not follow an established road but cut across open range, occasionally making a detour to travel wide of a ranch house or fenced claim. The two men ahead of him, and the man ahead of them, were all hugging the foothills. Quinn did not know exactly where a man would have swung to the left to follow the trail down through the Platte Valley, but he was pretty sure they had passed that point.

As he set his camp, he thought he could smell snow in the air. He thought that if the snow got very deep and he couldn't get ahead of Larkin and Cater the next day, he might pull out and go back to the Lockhart Ranch. He had been on the trail three days, and the two men he was following seemed to be traveling fast. Their trail rubbed out nearly all of the tracks that had been put down ahead of them, but Quinn had the general sense that Newman had started with a good lead and wasn't giving up much of it.

As Quinn snuggled into his blankets, all the

world was quiet. He expected a coyote wail, or a panther scream, or an owl hoot, but he heard nothing. It was too quiet.

Quinn awoke to the feel of a cold object against his nose. Opening his eyes, he saw it was a gun barrel. Kneeling over him and looking into his face was the man Larkin, dressed as always in the dark coat and hat, with the muffler wrapped around the lower half of his face. The upper part of his face was wrinkled and drawn, and the sunken yellow eyes moved in shadow.

Quinn's heart thumped in his chest, and his mouth was dry.

A voice came out of the hideous face. "I thought you was headed north."

"I was."

"Maybe you ought to go back there."

Quinn said nothing. He could see that the hammer was not cocked, and if Larkin had wanted to kill him he could have done so already. The man seemed more intent on scaring him.

"You don't know me," said the voice.

"We met. You said your name was Larkin. I told you my name was Quinn."

The muffler fell away, and the yellow teeth showed as the man's voice came up from his throat. "Quinn, quim. You don't know me, but I'm going to tell you who I am, so you'll know why you'd better go on and mind your own business."

"Go ahead."

"My name's Corbeau, boy. That's right. Clem Corbeau. Maybe you heard it before. My boy was

Ben. Uh-huh. Yer pal Slade, or Newman as you know him, double-crossed him."

"He was your boy?"

The man's lower lip trembled, and he clenched the yellow teeth. He opened his mouth to say, "He was," and then he locked his teeth again.

Quinn said nothing. His mouth was still dry, but his heartbeat had gone down.

"What d'you say to that?" the man growled as he jabbed the cold barrel into Quinn's nose.

"I don't have anything to say."

The gun barrel receded. "I guess not. Yer pal is a double-crossin' coward, that's all." Corbeau stood up, still holding the pistol in his hand. "That's why I'm justified. He double-crossed my boy."

Quinn gave a short nod. He could feel the wool cap still on his head.

"Yer friend Slade," Corbeau said with a sneer, "thinks he's smart. But there's somethin' he don't know."

"What's that?"

"He don't know who I am, so he don't know how strong my power is. When you know you're right, you're stronger. But he don't know me. If I get a chance, I'll tell him. But if he's dead by the time I get to him, an' he doesn't know who the bullet really come from, that's fine too. But it'll be mine. The bullet'll be mine." The man nodded, rocking on his heels. "The vengeance will be mine."

He cocked the pistol, and Quinn tensed. Then he let the hammer back down.

Quinn studied the troubled face. The man was

not tormenting him for enjoyment. He just wanted things in control—that was it. He couldn't shoot Quinn now, because it would throw everything out of balance. Quinn could see it in the yellow eyes. The man wanted Slade like other men wanted a meal or a drink or the softness of a woman. He didn't want anything else, and he didn't want to spoil what he hoped to have. He wanted to have it his way. Quinn could read it on his face.

The weather and the waiting must be getting to him, Quinn thought. The man wanted to get at Slade and he didn't want anyone in his way, but he couldn't catch up with one man while he was back here trying to put the fear of death into another one.

Corbeau brushed back the dark coat as he put the gun in his holster. "Go back home, boy," he said. "Stay out of this." Then he turned and walked away.

Quinn got up onto one elbow and watched the man go to his dark horse, which was standing ground-hitched with its reins on the ground. Corbeau gathered the reins, pulled himself into the saddle, and kicked the horse into a lope. Snow flew up behind the horse's hooves, and the muffled thuds faded as the horse took the dark rider out of sight.

Quinn sat up and shook the snow off his bedding. It had snowed about two inches, and flakes were still coming down. He was sure Corbeau was in a hurry to get on out ahead and try to close the gap on the man up ahead.

Quinn thought of turning back, as he had been advised to do, but he felt he had to see this thing through, at least for another day. He was not worried about Corbeau coming back after him, but he wondered what his chances were of getting ahead of the other two now.

The image of Corbeau came back to him. He felt a sick feeling in his stomach, a loathing, but he did not despise the man as he had before. If Corbeau was full of his own poison, at least he was justified in his own narrow view. Quinn could see that. He could also see that in a broader sense of justice, the man deserved a chance to go after the man who, in his view, had betrayed his son.

Thinking now of Newman, Quinn believed the man in the lead did not know who was after him. He would know he had to keep busy staying out in front, but he would not know who the dark figure was that was following him.

Quinn remembered Cater. He was still in the works somewhere. Corbeau had probably caught up with him by now, and they could well be planning on how to make their move today.

Everything seemed to be pushing forward. That was the feeling he had. He couldn't imagine Corbeau or even Cater hanging back at this point, just to intimidate him. He decided to keep following.

Back on the trail, Quinn followed Corbeau's tracks and in less than an hour came to the spot where Cater had waited for Corbeau. Quinn realized he had actually crept up on the other two at the close of the previous day. Now he could tell from the length of the horses' strides that Corbeau and Cater were moving straight out.

Snow was still falling, but the tracks were deep and the snowfall was not heavy. By late morning, Quinn thought he could make out a set of tracks beneath the trampling of the other two horses. It looked as if these were Newman's tracks from earlier in the day.

Quinn did a quick estimate. Newman might be four hours ahead of him, and two to three hours ahead of his pursuers. The gap was closing.

Quinn had had the good luck of observing Corbeau's tracks separately, so he could now distinguish between Corbeau's and Cater's hoofprints. When they rode side by side, Corbeau rode on the left. When they rode in single file, Cater went first.

It was a quiet day, gray and muffled with the snow still falling lightly. Once, at about midday, Quinn thought he heard a gunshot off in the south. He stopped the horse and listened for several long minutes, but he heard nothing more.

An hour later, he saw where the tracks diverged. Corbeau's tracks followed the main trail, and Cater's split off to the right. Quinn followed Cater's trail for half a mile to get an understanding. The horse had been moving fast, taking long strides and digging up dirt from beneath the snow. Quinn turned and headed back to the main trail. From the looks of it, the pursuers were making their play. Cater was going to give it a push and try to get ahead of Newman.

Quinn felt the tension building within himself.

The two men ahead of him were pushing, and Quinn felt himself getting caught up in it. He wanted to ride faster, get there sooner; but he told himself to take it easy on the horse. If the others wanted to ruin their horses, that was up to them. It didn't look as if Newman was going to let his horse get jaded, and that might be why the others were closing on him. Quinn raised his eyebrows. Maybe Newman was trying to get Corbeau and Cater to wear out their horses.

Quinn rode on. Occasionally he opened his mouth and tasted snowflakes, but it did very little good for his thirst. He had drunk the last of his water that morning, and he hadn't thought to fill his canteen when he watered his horse at the last creek. That was not clear thinking, he told himself. He was in too much of a hurry, and it could cause him to make a worse mistake.

The air was cold but humid with the falling snow, and he could smell the warm body of the horse. He took off his glove and touched the horse's neck; it was warm and slick. He knew why. Despite what he had told himself, he kept letting the horse out and then had to bring it back down to a walk.

Too fast, he thought. He was getting caught up in the frenzy. He had to slow down. It was early afternoon, and he had rested the horse very little. Now he had to keep from overheating it.

Somewhere up the trail, and he didn't know how far, there were two men trying to put the squeeze on a third one. He needed to be there, but he also needed to go easy on his horse. He made himself dismount and walk.

He was thirsty now, and he was sure the horse was, too. In an hour or two, or overnight, some horses could take in enough snow to meet their need for water. But that was a slow remedy for the present, and Quinn had never fully satisfied his own thirst by eating snow.

He walked for about half an hour, still following Corbeau's trail and, he imagined, Newman's. Finally he came to a small creek, one of several that he imagined ran into the Laramie River. He let the brown horse drink and then held him back. He walked the horse upstream until they came to a small, leafless tree. He tied the horse, then went to fill the canteen and quench his own thirst.

He waited for what he thought was twenty minutes, then untied the horse and let him drink again. When the horse lifted its drooling muzzle out of the water and looked at its master, Quinn thought they could move on. He felt the horse's neck, then its ribs behind the front shoulder. The sweat was dry.

Quinn stepped into the stirrup and was back on the trail. The largest peak of this mountain range, Laramie Peak, was behind him now, but large mountains still rose on his right. Somewhere down on the left and behind him was the town of Wheatland, and half a day's ride ahead was the town of Chugwater. In between the two towns, the trail forked—one way to Chugwater and

Cheyenne, and the other way to Rock River and Medicine Bow.

It was midafternoon now, and the sun was breaking through the clouds. The snow had let up, but a carpet of snow covered the countryside, and soft piles of it hung on very clump of sage-brush. The trail was still easy to read, as no one seemed to be slowing down.

Quinn felt the horse's neck. It felt fine. The horse was moving at a fast walk, breathing easy. It was a good horse. When it thought Quinn wanted to go fast, it worked hard. Now it knew he wanted to go slower. It was a good horse, too good a horse to run into the ground for this kind of business.

Quinn felt his mouth go dry again. He stopped the horse and drank from his canteen. He was about to let the horse go forward again as he strapped the canteen back onto the saddle, and then he stopped. He made himself take the time to tie on the canteen. Then he adjusted his reins and let the horse go forward.

Something had told him to slow down, and this time it wasn't just the smell of a warm horse. He didn't know what it was, but he felt it.

The horse walked on as before. The trail ran across the toes of several small ridges on this stretch, and some of the ridges had little cedar trees. The cedars, which had turned rust-colored for the winter, reflected the glow of the afternoon sun on one side and cast shadows on the other.

Ahead on the trail, a leafless cottonwood showed its upper branches where it stood down in a wash. It looked like a dead tree. It had the bark missing from most of its branches, and the dry, exposed limbs looked like weathered bones.

Two ravens sat in the upper branches, squawking to one another. Quinn rode forward, and more of the tree came into view. The ravens did not fly away until he came to the top of the rise, about fifty yards from the tree.

Now he could see the whole tree, from the exposed upper branches to the rough bark on the trunk.

A man sat against the trunk of the tree. Quinn thought he knew who it was, and he did not expect the man to look up.

Now the trail was on a level as it approached the tree. The man was sitting in the snow with his hands in his lap. The holster on his gunbelt was empty. His head was tipped forward, and Quinn could see a round-brimmed hat with a pinched peak in the crown.

Quinn stopped his horse and got down to look at the man. He saw the yellow hair, the full blond mustache, the drooping eyelids. He squatted further, and then he saw the small, round hole in the forehead. It looked like the size of hole that Newman's hideout gun would make.

Quinn stood up and looked at the slumped form. Cater must have really pushed the gray horse, and he must have been surprised. Quinn recalled Dexter saying that some people just weren't cut out for this country. The way things had turned out, it looked as if he might have been right.

Quinn backed up and looked again at the man sitting at the side of the trail. That was the way Newman would have done it. After he had made sure of Cater, he would have set him up on the trail for the other man to see. It might be Newman's idea of a joke. The first part probably wasn't. It would have been more like the time when Newman had shot the yellow dog. Quinn remembered his words. "I can finish what I start."

Chapter Sixteen

Quinn sloshed the cold water in his mouth, appreciating the taste even as he listened. He expected to hear gunshots any minute, but the world remained silent. Cater was behind him now, and ahead he saw only the rust-colored cedars standing like sentinels.

The encounter with the lifeless form of Cater had left Quinn with a new view of Newman. Up until now, Newman had seemed like a man who ran from his problems but had a lot of nerve. Now Quinn could put a finer point on it: Newman could kill a man.

Quinn thought through the time element again. It looked as if Newman had waited for Cater, which would have allowed Corbeau to close the distance between them. Newman might be waiting for Corbeau even now, instead of putting down more tracks. If Newman had slowed down, it wouldn't be until tomorrow that he took one trail to Cheyenne or the other to Rock River. Even if he had not slowed at all, he probably wouldn't make that move until late in the day today. It was more likely he was waiting to rimrock his other pursuer.

Quinn had his coat open now, and from time to time he touched the handle of his six-gun. He had the sense that things were bunching up now, with Newman directing his attention behind while Corbeau surged ahead. Quinn still did not think Corbeau would spoil his chance by lying in wait for Quinn while the main object was just ahead, but he thought it all might change if Corbeau got to Newman first. If Corbeau's chance paid off, he might then come back for Quinn.

The trail still followed the base of the mountains, which were lower now as the foothills fingered out into draws and dry washes. The trail ran steady, with only two sets of tracks now. Cater's horse had dropped out of the picture. It was probably standing up in a draw somewhere with its head down and its insides burned out, unless Newman had taken the trouble to put it down. Quinn wondered if he would have bothered, or if he would have seen it as a good measure to keep the remaining pursuer from having a second horse.

The sun was starting to drop in the west. It still hung well above the skyline of the mountains, but it would drop quickly now. Already the air was turning cooler.

Off to the south he heard a shot. He knew he heard it this time. First came the report, and then the echo as the sound carried out through the draws and canyons. Quinn stopped the horse and listened. A second shot followed from the same direction. Then came two more shots, spaced about fifteen seconds apart. All four sounded like rifle shots—long, forceful crashes and not the pop of a pistol as it would carry over a distance. Depending on what sort of land lay between, the shots would have come from no more than a couple of miles away.

It might be over, he thought. If he heard another flurry of shots he would know different. He waited for another long moment and then moved the horse forward.

He had his hand on the pistol butt half the time now. Shadows were stretching out from the sagebrush and low cedars. A couple of times it looked as if a shadow moved, but as he refocused, Quinn could tell it was his own vision, tired and jumpy from searching across snow and rocks and shadows.

He saw something on the trail up ahead, a dark form. Then it went out of sight as Quinn dipped into a draw. He came up the other side slowly, and as his line of vision cleared the crest he saw it was a horse. A dark horse, saddled but riderless, lay stretched out on the trail. It was facing Quinn, lying with its left side up. Quinn recognized the horse. It wasn't Cater's gray horse or Newman's dun. Quinn had seen the horse twice in the last four days—the two times he had seen Corbeau.

Riding closer, Quinn saw an empty rifle scabbard beneath the left stirrup fender. Corbeau must have gotten down on the ground and pulled his rifle. If he had made a good shot, he would want that scabbard to put on Newman's horse.

Quinn saw blood on the trail ahead. From the looks of it, the horse had taken a bullet and had run back the way it had come. Quinn had a pretty good idea now that Newman would have finished off Cater's horse as well.

The brown horse's nostrils quivered as it sidestepped around the fallen horse. Once around it, Quinn reined straight ahead and followed the trail for another quarter of a mile until he came to a low ridge.

He hesitated, then turned and followed the ridge uphill to the right, keeping himself out of view from whatever lay ahead. A hundred yards up the slope, the ground rose steeper toward the mountains. Quinn dismounted and walked slowly up to the crest he had been following on his left. He took off his hat and held it along with the reins in his left hand. His right hand was on the pistol butt.

Looking back down the slope to his left, he saw the area open up into a small basin a hundred yards across, a bowl of grass and sagebrush with a six-inch blanket of snow. In the center of the basin lay the dark form of Corbeau, facedown in the snow, with the black coat spread out like a cape. His hat, also dark against the snow, lay several yards away. The sun's rays were slanting now, and they reflected on the silver strands in the dark head of hair.

"Hello, Quinn." Newman's voice came from up above and to the right.

Quinn turned to locate him as Newman stepped into view from behind a jumble of rocks. He was wearing the tan jacket and carrying a rifle in his gloved hands. Quinn returned the greeting. "Hello."

Newman pointed the rifle in the direction of the sprawled body. "Sonofabitch came after me." Newman's eyes were hard as he looked at Quinn.

"Uh-huh."

"He didn't leave me much choice."

Quinn shrugged. "I'd guess not." He looked down at the body and thought, *At least Corbeau got his chance.*

Newman pointed again with the rifle. "I was up ahead, and he opened up on me. Then, after I dropped him, I come over here to wait and see if anyone else would come along."

Quinn nodded. "You must have got his horse with one of the shots." He motioned with his head. "It's dead on the trail back there a ways."

"I guess I did." Newman lifted his chin. "The two of 'em come after me. I didn't have one of these." He raised the rifle a couple of inches and then lowered it. "But lucky for me, Cater did."

Quinn looked in the direction of the dark body and then back at Newman. "Do you know who that is?"

Newman shook his head.

"Have you looked at him?"

"Not yet."

"Let's go do that," Quinn said.

"Just a minute." Newman went back to the rocks and came out with his horse. The fur coat was still tied to the front of the saddle.

The two men walked their horses down to the bottom where the dead man lay in the snow. Quinn could see that no footprints had come near the fallen body. He saw tracks leading out ahead, which matched with Newman's account that he was in the lead when the other man opened up on him. Quinn thought Newman might not have been in any hurry to see the man, but now they both stood over him.

The dead man lay in the snow, arms out-stretched, with a rifle sunk in the snow not far from his right hand. His head was turned to one side, and his eyes were closed. His nose and mouth were pressed into the snow, but his face was identifiable to Quinn.

"You don't know him?"

Newman shook his head.

"His name's Corbeau."

Newman had his lips pressed together, and he moved his head in a slight nod.

Quinn did not think it came as a great surprise. He went on. "He told me his name was Clem Corbeau, father of Ben. Slade's partner."

Newman flinched but said nothing.

"He told me he had justification for going after you."

258

Newman looked straight at Quinn. The blue eyes were hard. "He might have thought he did." The eyes flickered. "Did you come all the way here to tell me that?"

"That was part of it. But the more I got pulled into this, the more I knew I needed to ask you a question."

Newman looked around at the cold, silent surroundings. "Go ahead and shoot. Ain't nobody here but us two."

"Did he?"

"Did he what?"

"Did he have justification?"

Newman cocked his eyebrows. "I rode with a partner once, with a name you just mentioned, and when he got shot up I had to leave him. But I didn't finish him off, not like someone said. He was in bad shape, which he had to be if he was dead when the posse got to him."

"But he was alive when you left him?"

"Yeh, but he couldn't ride any more."

Quinn took a deep breath. "What did he say before you left?" He imagined the man staying game, telling his partner to ride for it.

Newman gave a small shake to his head. "Nothing."

Quinn imagined the man's feeling of being lost, the sinking feeling that he was being left to die alone. He looked at Newman. "And you took the horse."

Newman was stone-faced. "I had to."

Quinn could see it. A change of horses would

259

have made the difference, and the man who got away wouldn't have seen where he had done any great wrong.

Newman spoke again. "You've got to look out for yourself. No one else is goin' to. You said it yourself, Quinn. A man's got to be careful."

Quinn felt himself flare up. "But I was lookin' out for you."

"When you told me that?"

"That, and when I took out after you on this wild-goose chase."

Newman coughed and shook his head. "You didn't have to go to all that bother. You could have got yourself hurt for nothin'."

That was the way it was going to be, Quinn thought. Not a word of thanks. If anything, Newman thought he was a fool for not looking out for himself.

Newman turned and walked away, leading his horse and carrying the rifle. He stopped a few yards up the trail and turned, as if he had just wanted to get a ways away from the body. He had the rifle and the reins both in his left hand.

Quinn led his horse over to the place where Newman stood. "Well, I guess I'm done here, then," he said.

Newman turned down the corners of his mouth, looked around, and nodded. "I'd say. Everything's done."

Quinn put out his hand. "So long, Newman."

The corners of Newman's mouth turned up as he put out his right hand. "So long, Quinn. It's been good to know you."

"Good luck."

"And the same to you, Quinn." Newman tossed the rifle in the snow, checked his rigging, and stepped up into the saddle. He touched his hat brim and rode away.

Quinn let out a long sigh as he checked his own cinch. He realized he had called the man Newman and thought of him as Newman right up to the end. But he was Slade, all right—the man who took his part out of the middle and let everyone else pick up the pieces. Now he was gone, and Quinn did not want to know if he was headed to Cheyenne or out through the Sybille, or if he was going somewhere to meet someone.

Daylight was fading now, and dusk was setting in. Long shadows were stretching across the blue-gray snow of evening. Quinn wanted to be on his way. This was Slade's mess and not his. He decided he would drop down from the foothills and take the main trail back north. He could have a campfire tonight and make coffee for the first time on this trip.

He swung into the saddle and looked across the cold country to the north. Life was not perfect where he was headed, but he had seen enough to know it was better than what he had been through. There was still such a thing as friendship, even if he had missed out on it this time. He recalled Dexter reading a letter for Sipe and then helping him write one in return. Not everyone was a lone coyote or had to be.

He could make it through the winter until he got put on wages again. He could stay on awhile at the Lockhart, where people at least gave a damn about each other. He could cut firewood for Moose and do a few other odd jobs to earn his keep, and he could fill in a fourth hand at cards.

He could also pay a visit now and then to a little ranch house up by Lost Spring. There was a woman he would like to get to know better—a woman who believed in trust and who would have some ideas on how to take the bitter with the sweet.

TROUBLE MAN

ED GORMAN

Ray Coyle used to be a gunfighter. And when he gets word his boy has been killed in a gunfight in Coopersville, he has to go there—to bring the body home. But when the old gunfighter steps off the train, he brings his gun with him, along with something else . . . trouble.

___4440-4 $4.99 US/$5.99 CAN

ZANE GREY

RANGERS OF THE LONE STAR

Deputy Marshal Russ Sittell is on special assignment from the Texas Rangers to work with Vaughan Steele in putting a stop to the rampant rustling in Pecos County. But everyone knows that local rancher—and mayor—Granger Longstreth doesn't want any Ranger interference in his town. When Russ takes a job on Longstreth's ranch, he's able to learn exactly how the rancher operates—and he witnesses the growing tension between Longstreth and Steele. A tension that can lead only to trouble.

___4556-7 $4.99 US/$5.99 CAN

BITTER TRUMPET

FRED GROVE

Jesse Wilder survived the hell of a Yankee prison camp and the shame of volunteering for the Union Army of the West—the only way to escape certain death in the camp. But when the war ends and he comes home to Tennessee, word of his "treachery" precedes him, and Jesse finds himself shunned by his neighbors and disinherited by his father. Jesse drifts west, and in El Paso his drifting stops. There he meets Cullen Floyd, who runs weapons across the border to the Juaristas in Mexico. Cullen needs another gun against the marauding Apaches and the murderous banditos. Jesse needs a job. Before he knows it, Jesse is caught up in another desperate struggle, this time against the trained mercenaries of the Emperor Maximilian. But Jesse may have pushed his luck too far—this is one battle he may not survive.

___4616-4 $4.50 US/$5.50 CAN

Dorchester Publishing Co., Inc.
P.O. Box 6640
Wayne, PA 19087-8640

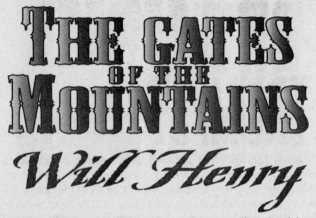

THE GATES OF THE MOUNTAINS

Will Henry

President Thomas Jefferson buys the sprawling Louisiana Territory from the French, and it is left to the team of Meriwether Lewis and William Clark to hoist the Stars and Stripes over the distant northwestern frontier and win an empire with three small boats and forty ragged volunteers. Among them is novice boatman Francois Rivet, half French and half Pawnee. Young Rivet is on a quest of his own, no less fraught with danger—a search for his long-lost father held captive by the Shoshone Indians. But this trek into the vast unknown holds more than a few perils and surprises for them all.

___4653-9 $4.99 US/$5.99 CAN

BRANDISH

DOUGLAS HIRT

FIRST TIME IN PAPERBACK!

Captain Ethan Brandish has finally given up his command of Fort Lowell, deep in Apache territory. But the vicious Apache leader, Yellow Shirt, has another fate in store for him. He and a group of renegade warriors attack a stage station and ride off just before Brandish arrives. But the Apaches are still out there—watching and waiting—and Brandish must risk his own life to save the few wounded survivors.

___4323-8 $4.50 US/$5.50 CAN

Dorchester Publishing Co., Inc.
P.O. Box 6640
Wayne, PA 19087-8640

Please add $1.75 for shipping and handling for the first book and $.50 for each book thereafter. NY, NYC, and PA residents, please add appropriate sales tax. No cash, stamps, or C.O.D.s. All orders shipped within 6 weeks via postal service book rate. Canadian orders require $2.00 extra postage and must be paid in U.S. dollars through a U.S. banking facility.

Name_____
Address_____
City_____State_____Zip_____
I have enclosed $_____ in payment for the checked book(s).
Payment <u>must</u> accompany all orders. ☐ Please send a free catalog.

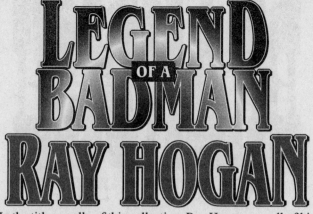

LEGEND OF A BADMAN

RAY HOGAN

In the title novella of this collection, Ray Hogan uses all of his storytelling powers and his keen eye for character to recreate the life and times of frontiersman Clay Allison. Hogan looks beyond the rowdy reputation and past the gunfights to portray a man of integrity, willing to put his life on the line for what he believes in. Was Allison a western Robin Hood, defending the poor and weak? Was he a vicious killer who gunned down more than twenty men? Or is the truth somewhere in between? In this masterful tale, Ray Hogan presents not the rumors, but the truth—not the myth, but the man.

___4560-5 $4.50 US/$5.50 CAN

DARK TRAIL

Hiram King

When the War Between the States was finally over, many men returned from battle only to find their homes destroyed and their families scattered to the wind. Bodie Johnson is one of those men. But while some families fled before advancing armies, the Johnson family was packed up like cattle and shipped west—on a slave train. With only that information to go on, Bodie sets out to find whatever remains of his family. And he will do it. Because no matter how vast the West is, no matter what stands in his way, Bodie knows one thing—the Johnsons will survive.

___4418-8 $5.50 US/$6.50 CAN

KIT CARSON

BLOOD RENDEZVOUS
DOUG HAWKINS

The high point of any trapper's year is the summer rendezvous, the annual gathering where mountain men from all over the frontier meet to trade the pelts they risked their lives for. But for Kit Carson, the real danger lies in getting to the rendezvous. He is leading a party of trappers, all of them weighed down with a year's worth of furs. That is enough to make them a tempting target for any killer on the trail—especially when the trail leads through Blackfoot territory.

___4499-4 $3.99 US/$4.99 CAN

Last Chance

DEE MARVINE

Mattie Hamil is on a frantic journey west. On her own, with only her grit and determination to see her through, she has to find her charming gambler of a fiancé, and she has to do it fast—before her pregnancy shows. From a steamboat along the Missouri River to the rough-and-tumble post-gold-rush town of Last Chance, Montana, Mattie's trek leads her through danger and sorrow, friendship and joy. But even after she finds her fiancé, no bend in the trail leads to what she expected.

___4475-7 $4.99 US/$5.99 CAN

Dorchester Publishing Co., Inc.
P.O. Box 6640
Wayne, PA 19087-8640

Please add $1.75 for shipping and handling for the first book and $.50 for each book thereafter. NY, NYC, and PA residents, please add appropriate sales tax. No cash, stamps, or C.O.D.s. All orders shipped within 6 weeks via postal service book rate. Canadian orders require $2.00 extra postage and must be paid in U.S. dollars through a U.S. banking facility.

Name_____
Address_____
City_____ State_____ Zip_____
I have enclosed $_____ in payment for the checked book(s).
Payment <u>must</u> accompany all orders. ❑ Please send a free catalog.
    CHECK OUT OUR WEBSITE! www.dorchesterpub.com